Zane's Sex Chronicles

Also by Zane

Dear G-Spot: Straight Talk about Sex and Love

Love Is Never Painless

Afterburn

The Sisters of APF: The Indoctrination of Soror Ride Dick

Nervous

Skyscraper

The Heat Seekers

Gettin' Buck Wild: Sex Chronicles II

The Sex Chronicles: Shattering the Myth

Shame on It All

Addicted

Edited by Zane

Succulent: Chocolate Flava II

Caramel Flava: The Eroticanoir.com Anthology

Chocolate Flava: The Eroticanoir.com Anthology

Breaking the Cycle

Blackgentlemen.com

Sistergirls.com

Zane's Sex Chronicles

Zane

ATRIA BOOKS

New York London Toronto Sydney

ATRIA BOOKS
A Division of Simon & Schuster, Inc.
1230 Avenue of the Americas
New York, NY 10020

ATRIA BOOKS and colophon are trademarks
of Simon & Schuster, Inc.

Manufactured in the United States of America

ISBN: 978-0-7394-9878-1

*This book is dedicated to Suzanne de Passe
for being a fabulous woman, a legend, and a wonderful mentor*

Contents

Introduction

It has been a long road getting here, but every day of this journey has been a gift. As a child, I grew to have a love of the cultural arts. My parents encouraged it by constantly taking my siblings and me to plays, museums, and art galleries. We traveled quite a bit, and our parents taught us that the world is a big place and that variety is the spice of life.

Even though much of what I learned was taught outside of our home, my greatest joys were books and television. They were a way for me to escape boredom and live my life vicariously through the eyes, actions, and words of others. I was intrigued by the characters and the way stories played out, whether throughout the pages of a book or on the screen.

My mother signed me up for speed reading when I was in the third grade. By the sixth grade, I was reading a book a day. Part of it was my competitive spirit back then. All of my siblings had skipped one or two grades, and I was the youngest, so I had much to prove with both parents being educators. We had a second basement in my childhood home—called "the Study"—that had literally thousands of books lining all the walls. Over the years, my father has collected more than eight thousand titles on theology and psychology alone. I loved reading, even back then, and I could never quench my thirst for knowledge. To this day, I read a ton of self-help books every year to improve my quality of life.

Yet and still, I found time for my favorite shows, many of which today's youth would not know about. A lot of the male characters on television were enjoyable and interesting, but the strong female characters fascinated me to no end. Lucille Ball had me in stitches during every episode of *I Love Lucy.* I cried like a baby the day she passed away, not only because of her talent but also because of the way she had lived her life and made the most of every moment.

Florida Evans, the matriarch of *Good Times,* was the bomb diggity, and Thelma and Willona were a couple of tough, vibrant sisters. I am now blessed to call BernNadette Stanis, who portrayed Thelma, a friend. She was the first major crush for many young African-American males of that era and they flock to her today at book signings for her relationship book *Situations 101.* She still looks phenomenal.

Who could forget the strong female presence on *The Jeffersons, Maude, Dynasty, Knots Landing, Dallas,* and *What's*

Happening!! Yes, I was caught up, even in cartoons. Even Wilma Flintstone and Betty Rubble had it going on. Sure, there were men on the shows. I will not tell a lie. Philip Michael Thomas was my first major crush. It was a tie between him and Prince, who sexually liberated me through his music. That's another story for another day. If you have read my books, then you already know I have the hots for Prince. As for *Miami Vice* and Philip Michael Thomas, I never missed an episode. I watched it while I was in labor with my first son; ten minutes before they cut my stomach open and pulled him out I was feenin for Philip's ass.

All of this is to say that while books are my first love, I am so excited to be able to segue into the world of television. I have four TiVos in my crib and now I can tape my own show. How hot is that?

While *Zane's Sex Chronicles* is for both sexes, we already know that men are going to tune in to any show with the word "sex" in the title. However, I did not want the show that bears my name to be about sexual exploitation. Like my books, *Zane's Sex Chronicles* is about empowerment and liberation—both in and out of the bedroom. It is about realizing that women are not missionaries for the pleasure of men. We are their equals.

If I have said it once, I have said it a hundred times. It is time for the sexual revolution. I am not saying go out and jump on every dick—available or not—and have a free-for-all. Although if that is what you want to do, that is certainly your business. I am simply encouraging you to enjoy every aspect of life, which includes making love. Whether you are in a heterosexual relationship, a same-gender loving relationship or a combination of the two, make your desires known. Our lovers are only as good as we are. No one is psychic and everyone's sexual triggers are different.

All five of the main characters of *Zane's Sex Chronicles* are unique in their own right and they deal with common day-to-day issues that all women must deal with, along with a lot of freaky-ass shit because I created them. Patience James aka Zane, Maricruz, Lyric, Eboni, and Ana Marie are a force to be reckoned with. I hope that as they grow, you will grow. I hope that their lives will become the topic of office, watercooler, hair salon, and barbershop discussions. Them and their fine-ass men, because we do have plenty of those on the show as well.

Now here comes the part where I ask for your help. Hell, I am like the Temptations: I "Ain't Too Proud to Beg." I want to prove that an urban erotic series can blow up the spot on cable television. I want the highest-rated show that they have ever had. I love most of the violent, gang-banging prison shows just as much as the next person and wear out my TiVos taping them. Now let's show the world that we are sexy, that we are loving. I don't simply want you to watch *Zane's Sex Chronicles*. I want you and everyone you know to watch it. Have your friends over for a *Zane's Sex Chronicles* party. Take turns hosting them for each weekly episode. Whether you bring your men with you or leave them at home, that's up to you, but have some fun with it.

I know that most of you do not believe in chain letters, but I swear, if you don't email at least fifty people within an hour after you read this introduction and tell them to send a blank email to eroticanoir-subscribe@topica.com to join my email list, you will never have another orgasm in your entire life. Don't believe me? Fail to do it and see what happens. <smile> Seriously, I want a million people on my email list by the end of this year. Okay, two or three million. So please help spread the word and ask everyone to join my list so they can participate in all the contests, keep informed, and enjoy life with me because I am just getting started.

Meanwhile, as a tribute to the series, I have decided to release this "tie-in" book that contains the stories featured in the first season of *Zane's Sex Chronicles*. I hope that you enjoy them.

Make sure that you visit me online at www.eroticanoir .com, and if you MySpace—and who the hell doesn't?— you can find me at www.myspace.com/zaneland, where you can interact with me on my blog. No topic is too scandalous or taboo for me to talk about, that's for damn sure. Tell me how you like the show by posting on the discussion boards or joining the live chat during each episode. Thanks again for all of the support that you have given me. You are all truly loved and appreciated.

Blessings,

Zane

Zane's Sex Chronicles

Patience James

My life is complicated. It's complicated, stressful and, oftentimes, overwhelming, but I would not trade it for anything in the world. Men have not made it any easier. I do not know if they are taught the "macking game" in elementary school, but by the time most boys reach high school, their main objectives in life are getting paid and making sure that girls get played. The first boy ever to break my heart was named Kevin. Two years after he made me want to evaporate after embarrassing me in the hallway at school when he dumped me for Claire, I looked back on it and wondered what I had ever seen in his ass. I graduated from high school having had three serious relationships and many others that lasted no more than a few weeks and consisted of a bunch of late-night phone calls, provocative talk that led absolutely nowhere, and not a single real date.

I have always had the gift of gab, as my mother calls it. She claims that I came out of the womb ready to shout,

kick ass, and take names. It is true that I am the most determined person I know. My family calls me stubborn and
I have no problem claiming that, if stubborn means that I
want to achieve my goals in life. Failure is not an option for
me, and I come from a family full of people who share a
similar strength of mind. Sometimes it can be like the clash
of the titans in the James household, but everyone is always
supportive of one another.

From an early age, I knew that I would end up doing
something that involved convincing others to do something. As it turned out, during my senior year of college,
I got an intern position at Flava Cosmetics. That was the
big break that I was looking for, and I was determined
to impress everyone from the CEO to the receptionist. I
strutted into the office like I owned the joint from day one.
I had all sorts of marketing ideas for the various cosmetic
lines, and people loved them, everyone except for Kerrigan, but that is a different story for a different day. Let's
just say that Kerrigan is the thorn in my side, but the majority of the time I pay no heed to the ignoramus. We have
our moments, but it is all good in competition. It helps to
keep me on my toes.

Kerrigan does not realize that women need a different
slant on marketing from men. Men will be satisfied with
half-naked women in ads looking like they want to fuck
the living daylights out of somebody. Yes, sexuality can go a
long way in advertisements, but "sensuality" can go a whole
lot farther. Women do not want to feel threatened when
they look at ads. In other words, women want to see adver-

tisements featuring women who look like them, not some impossible dream version of them. A lot of companies, like Dove soap, are catching on by embracing normal-looking women in their ads and commercials. Average women, especially women of color, are not a size four and do not look like they stepped out of *Playboy*. They look . . . normal.

Let me quit talking about my job. You can see that I am passionate about it, and that is what matters in life: being passionate about what you do—and whom you love.

Love. That can be a good or dirty word for me, depending on the time period in my life. I have had many good men in my life, but all of them eventually faltered and none of them appreciated me until I was history. Devon wanted to control me. I was not then nor am I now the one for that. William had a big heart but he also had a big recreational drug problem. He had to go, but we remain friends. Lincoln was my cheater, the man who wanted to be in a committed relationship without actually making a commitment. I am sure he is somewhere, at this very second, trying to convince a sister to drop her drawers.

Lincoln, ironically since he was the one trying to fuck everything moving, was the most difficult to get rid of. He was so full of himself and so conceited that he never fathomed that I would dump him after he cheated. To this day, he still emails me and even tried to get me to join his network on Facebook. No way, not me. Lincoln broke the cardinal rule: he tried to creep out on me during Christmastime. Every real player knows that you keep your ass home on holidays. He tried to make me believe that he was meeting his best friend, Chris, in Denver to go skiing. Lincoln's ass had never been anywhere near a ski, rather less a slope. When a massive snowstorm hit and the Denver airport was shut down, he still insisted on going, stating that he did not want to disappoint Chris and that the airport would probably open back up. His stupid ass ended up stranded in the Chicago airport on a layover for two days. Dummy. He finally made it back home with his tail tucked between his legs. By that time, I had gone through his cell phone bills and, lo and behold, he had been conversing with some hooker candidate named Bonnie for months. He had been sweating pussy on the internet, surely having met her on MySpace where he spent hours a day, and was trying to go collect his award for putting in so much email and phone time.

I really should not call Bonnie a hooker candidate since I don't know her. She is probably some woman suffering from low self-esteem who can't find a local man to save her life so she fell for Lincoln's okey-doke. A lot of people go on the internet to flirt and call it a day. However, in today's time, the internet has become a breeding ground for more than pedophiles. It is a breeding ground for adults seeking out dick and pussy all over the globe.

I must admit that I found it fascinating, which is how my "double life" first came about. I went into a chat room a couple of years ago and even though my profile was a skeleton with nothing intriguing to make someone approach me, men instantly starting blowing up my screen with instant messages. They would ask my name, and there was not a chance in hell that I was going to say that I was Patience James. That is when "Zane" was born. I had always thought that name sounded cool. Later I found out that it means "God's gracious gift." I embrace every day above-ground as a gift so it actually fits me to some degree, even though the selection for that reason was unintentional.

I met this guy named Marshall in a chat room. He was from Atlanta and we started flirting. Then he asked me to "cyber," and I had no clue what he was talking about until he sent me a link to a private room and started typing shit about blowing my back out. I thought it was hilarious and wondered if he was actually getting off on the other side of his computer. I played along and typed all kinds of nasty things, about licking him from head to toe and riding his dick. He asked for my number, and that was when I exited the room. Not the kid. Marshall could have been an ax murderer and I was not about to find out. Granted, I was kind of in the middle of a dick drought at the time. Not because I could not find any men to take me to bed but because when I allowed it, they either disappointed me by not living up to my fantasies or they broke my zero-bullshit-tolerance policy and did or said something stupid.

Some women do not mind a man saying things to them like, "You can't control this dick!" or "I can get pussy when I can't get sleep!" I find that to be totally disrespectful and will not occupy my time with Jerry Springer nonsense. I watch the show because it lets me know how many women are really stressing over men who probably would not spit on them if their asses were on fire. I realized that there are a ton of women who are completely confused about relationships and their sensuality. So . . . I started writing my fantasies on the computer. Stories about hot, enticing relationships where feelings and efforts are reciprocated.

The first story that I ever wrote was called "First Night." I fantasized about meeting up with that fellow Marshall, whom I had cybered with but would not give my phone number. We rode up the coast of Maine on the back of a motorcycle, checked into a romantic bed-and-breakfast, and made love on the balcony. I posted it on my free web page provided by my internet host and people went absolutely bananas. Strangers started emailing me, asking to be put on my mailing list. They said it was the hottest shit they had ever read. I thought it was amusing and wrote two more stories, "The Seduction" and "The Airport." Within three weeks, I had eight thousand hits from word-of-mouth before my provider took the pages down for vulgarity. From there, I moved on to posting stories on the ACLU Black Erotica Board, where I met a lot of fellow erotica writers. We became friends, albeit only via email. I was Zane and they were whatever fake name they were using.

Eventually I started Eroticanoir.com, my home away from home, where I now post stories, answer advice mail, and do a monthly e-zine called *The Sex Chronicles*. Blogging came along, and now I find myself posting whatever, whenever, so that I can get an immediate reaction from people. I might vent about anything from my favorite subject—women being undervalued in society—to spawning discussions on whether or not pussy juice is left on the poles at strip clubs when the next dancer comes out. Like I said, I have the gift of gab. Being able to communicate with strangers from around the world excites me. I can say off-the-wall things that I would never say to my friends or family. Speaking of which, none of them know that I am Zane. They talk about Zane all the time, though, even my coworkers. "Have you read her latest blog, Patience?" "Patience, isn't Zane's shit hot?" "Patience, I'm going to write Zane for advice." "I can't wait to try that shit from Zane's story on my man!"

Not only do they have no clue that I am Zane, they act like I have damn near committed a crime by refusing to buy into the entire thing and read her work. Even the men that I have dated since I became "the Queen of Erotica" do not know that I am Zane. However, Patience and Zane share a lot of the same characteristics. We both believe that if women are going to have sex, and most will at some point in their lives, there is no reason for them to walk away from the experiences any less satisfied than the men. We both believe that there is something wrong in a society when the main sexual position is referred to as the missionary, as if we are merely vessels for a man's pleasure.

Honestly, I believe that if men could fuck themselves, they would see no need for women altogether. We are seriously undervalued in society, even though in many households the women are bringing home the majority of the bacon. I have friends who are lawyers and doctors and their men expect them to carry a heavy workload and still have dinner on the table every night. Their men refuse to help drop off and pick up the kids from school, take them to extracurricular activities, or even wash their own damn drawers. I get tons of mail asking for advice, and most of them are from women. A lot of them are sex related, like failure to have an orgasm *ever* to being scared to ride a man's dick to wanting to know how to give a decent blow job. Yet, hands down, most of them deal with relationship drama, and many of the women know in their gut what is really going on; they just need another woman to validate it and they are too embarrassed to talk to their friends or——more important——the person they are in the relationship with. Lack of communication is the downfall of most relationships.

To all the women in the world out there reading this, let me make something clear: You have nothing to be embarrassed about. A thief is always going to be a thief, no matter what situation you put him in. A con artist is always going to be a con artist and a doggish-ass man is always going to be a doggish-ass man. Nine times out of ten, men do not hurt women because the women deserve it. Men hurt women because the world is full of damaged people inflicting pain on other damaged people. Similarly, a lot of women seek out men to hurt, but women tend to do it in another fashion. Women try to withhold sex, which is asinine because the men will go handle their business elsewhere. If you get to the point in a relationship where you feel you have to clamp your legs shut to get him to behave, the relationship is already over. The imminent breakup is merely a formality. The same goes for suspicion of cheating. When two people truly love each other, they will not do anything that can even be misconstrued as cheating. If you find yourself searching pants pockets or reading emails or—in the case of me with Lincoln—scanning cell phone bills, your shit is already over.

I could go on and on, but I will refrain. I do enough of that on Eroticanoir.com so if you really want to hear me vent, log on. Off-line, I have a set of friends that I adore more than life itself. I try to help them out as much as possible, but I am not a psychiatrist. I have known Lyric and Ana Marie since high school. Lyric has a wonderful husband, Estaban, but certain strains are taking a toll on their relationship. Over time, I believe that they will work things out because I have never seen a couple more in love. They share a medical practice and need to reignite a few sparks here and there, but it will be all good.

Ana Marie is hooked up with Taariq and I have mixed feelings about those two. They seem to care for one another, but both of them are struggling entertainers and money is always running low. I believe in pursuing a dream, but you should never lose sight of the fact that you have to pay bills. They could work regular jobs and still do the comedy thing (in Ana Marie's case) and the rap thing (in Taariq's case) until something breaks.

Maricruz works with me at Flava. I wish I had a magic

wand that I could wave in front of her face and make her realize that she deserves better. Maricruz is still caught up with her ex-husband, a disrespectful poodle—he is not man enough to be a pit bull—who is shacking with another woman but still thinks Maricruz belongs to him. In many ways, she does. Her family is old-fashioned and does not believe in divorce. At least she got over that hump and legally got rid of him. Other than that, though, they might as well still be married because she is at his beck and call when it comes to giving up some pussy. Granted they have two kids, but he never took that into consideration when he started banging Stacy. I am getting too overheated, merely by typing this, so I better move on.

I met Eboni at an expo. Some "manwhore" named Raphael was dogging her out in front of everybody. I distracted her and told her to—in a nutshell—"fuck him," and we have been tight ever since. Eboni is originally from Little Rock, Arkansas, and her family is as traditional as they come. Her father thinks men should be working and women should be in the kitchen, barefoot and pregnant. Eboni decided to break camp right out of high school, and I admire the fact that she never went back. She was determined to start her own business, make her way in life, and she struggled until she got there. On a sour note, I will mention that she believes in using several men to satisfy her sexual needs. I do not think that she can ever truly find a good man until she realizes that satisfaction is more about quality and not quantity.

As for me, I am not sure what I want when it comes

to a man. I know that I want him to be attentive but not overbearing, compassionate but not hostile, appreciative but not an ass kisser, goal oriented but not a workaholic, attractive but not so metrosexual that I have to fight him for mirror time. Damn, maybe I do know what I want in a man. The only question is: Does such a man exist?

Ana Marie Hawkings

I met Taariq at the end of one of the darkest, most trying time periods of my life. If it were not for my girls, especially Patience and Lyric whom I go way back with, I would not have made it through it at all. I only wish that I had been honest with them sooner, instead of hiding the truth like an idiot.

When I was a little girl, I never aspired to sell my pussy. The exact opposite. I wanted to get married young, have a ton of babies, and be fat and sitting in a rocking chair by the time I was sixty with my husband of forty-plus years sitting right beside me. But just like everyone else, life has thrown me a bunch of curveballs. I had a rough childhood. I know, I know. People use that as an excuse all the time and I am no different. I did have a rough childhood, and those experiences laid the foundation for what I was to become.

My father—if you can even use that word to refer to him—left my mother to raise three kids alone without blinking an eye. I wonder if we have ever even been an afterthought since he walked out that door when I was twelve. I was the oldest. My younger siblings, a set of female twins, were only five. Momma busted her ass as a waitress, working for scraps, both the monetary kind and the food kind. Our dinner every night consisted of whatever had been burned by mistake or was about to be tossed in the trash for the winos to shuffle through. All of it was laden with fat, and by the time I was fifteen, I was overweight. Everyone teased me, except for Patience and Lyric, my best friends since elementary school.

They started sneaking fruit and vegetables out of their homes, after their mothers went grocery shopping, and bringing them over to my apartment so we could eat healthier. Patience could see that I was getting depressed about my weight so we started running three days a week and working out at the YWCA the other two. Within a year, I was the finest thing walking down the hallway at school.

Everything happens for a reason, though. During that year, when I was getting teased and bullied, I fought back with humor. If people could not appreciate me for my looks, I was determined to kill them with laughter. I got into trouble in a lot of my classes by taking up too much class time with my jokes. Some of them I had heard here or there but, even back then, I was making up most of my own material. It was Lyric who encouraged me actually to pursue a career in comedy. Patience was on the fence. She felt that I should go to college, but with my grades and coming from a family without two nickels to rub together, even if I took out loans,

I was not trying to get stuck with paying interest on them for the next ten to twenty years. School was not for me. It is not that I am not smart, but I am not book smart and I prefer simply to live my life to the fullest.

That sentiment is what probably got me into trouble. As I pursued a career in comedy right out of high school, I fell in with the wrong crowd. I experimented with a lot of drugs but, thank goodness and through the grace of God, I managed not to get addicted to any of them. Yet and still, the times that I was out of it because of whatever drug of choice was running through my system, I started doing stupid things. I had sex with a lot of men for a lot of reasons, mostly because of searching for the love I never got from my father. Over time, as my comedy career struggled to stay afloat, I began having sex for money. I figured what the hell. Women all over the world give up pussy for free. I might as well get something out of it.

I enjoy sex, always have. It is a stress reliever for me. It helps me calm down after a crazy night on the circuit. I am good at some things, even better at others, but I am off the chain when it comes down to fucking. Men will pay a sister to do what their wives and girlfriends think is beneath them. Things they are too afraid to do, too ashamed to do, or feel they do not have to do because they assume their pussies are lined with gold.

I needed the money, not only to support myself but also to help out my mother and younger sisters. Momma had made sacrifices in order to raise us, and if I had to make sacrifices to make her life a little easier, then that was what

I was going to do. Sure, I realized that Patience and Lyric
would have helped me out, set me up with a nine-to-five,
or whatever. That was not my cup of tea and still is not to
this day. I love comedy. I love being up late at night, hanging out at clubs, being around the in-crowd, and taking
each day as it comes.

I had it all planned out. I would sell some ass whenever
I needed some funds, wanted to have fun, or a combination of the two. I was appearing regularly at about half a
dozen comedy clubs around town. The money was nothing
to brag about but, combined with the money I was making from servicing men, I did all right. Now, do not get
it twisted. I have never been a streetwalker. Nor was I a
high-class call girl who chilled up in a penthouse and had
my clientele shower me with gifts. I was somewhere in
between. I had regular clients, all of whom I had met when
I was hanging out somewhere getting into something. Yes, I
had it all planned out until . . .

. . . I met Taariq. The second I laid eyes on him, I knew
he was my future. I had been in "minor" relationships over
the years but nothing committed. It was Open Mike Night
at Proud Mary's. They held it the third Wednesday of every
month. Normally I would not have even been around, but
my regular gig had been canceled, so I decided to cruise
through and see what was happening. I was so used to being
up half the night that being in my apartment would have
driven me insane.

Taariq was the third person to perform, right after a
poetess and a saxophone player who had a serious future in

front of him if the right person ever heard him play. Taariq came out and started rapping about sex. His smooth voice, which matched his smooth caramel skin, had me and every other woman in the place mesmerized. He spoke of licking whipped cream from between toes and giving candlelit bubble baths and full-body massages. He spoke of romantic evenings walking along the beach and sipping champagne from the same glass and rocking a sister's world. I was thinking, "Damn! Damn! Damn!" as my panties became saturated with my pussy juice.

After his set, I decided to play it cool. I could tell by the way women were oohing and aahing that somebody was going to make a play for him. I sat by the bar and observed as he shot down chica after chica. But . . . he was eyeing me. I felt him feeling me. I gave him the eye. You know the eye. The way a woman looks at a man when she wants to know if he wants to make some magic. Quite frankly, I grew disappointed over the next hour, the amount of time it took the rest of the people to perform. Taariq never walked my way.

I told the bartender to settle up my tab on my credit card and I was about to bounce. I sucked in some air, disgusted that after all the experience I had macking men and fucking the living daylights out of them, Taariq had me somewhat intimidated. Too intimidated to approach the man of my dreams. Also, I would be lying not to admit that, in the back of my mind, I was wondering how I could ever balance a relationship—which I knew that I would crave with him— and my extracurricular activity of fucking for pay.

By the time I hit the parking lot and pressed the unlock button on my key ring, Taariq was behind me saying, "Leaving so soon?"

Even in a big city, sometimes the world can seem like an extremely small place. With just the two of us in the parking lot, everything and everyone else disappeared in my mind. "I have an early day tomorrow," I lied. "Besides, the show ended awhile back. You were very good, by the way."

"Thanks. I wrote that song for someone I know." He paused. "I mean, someone I used to know."

I grinned in discomfort. "Well, whoever she is, she is a very lucky woman to have brought out such passion in your lyrics."

Taariq shrugged. "Obviously she didn't see it that way. She ran off and married my cousin."

"Sorry to hear that."

"He's a trifling ass and she's even more trifling. Now they're off somewhere, leading a trifling life."

I could see the pain in his eyes and hear it in his voice, even though I did not know him at all, rather less well enough to gauge his expressions. Yet, people who have been hurt recognize it.

"So why did you follow me out to the parking lot?" I asked, hoping to change the subject and get at least a phone number before I jetted.

"I was feeling you all night," Taariq replied. "I didn't want to risk the chance of never seeing you again."

I snickered. "I had no clue. I was feeling you also but,

after watching you swat down all those other women, I didn't think I had a shot."

"Shit, as fine as you are, baby girl, you can shoot at the moon and hit a bull's-eye on that motherfucker!"

There is something about a roughneck that turns my ass on. My panties were getting drenched all over again. Taariq licked his lips and I almost fainted. No man had ever had that instant effect on me before. I wanted to throw him on the hood of my car and fuck him to death or die trying.

"Baby girl, let's go grab a late-night drink someplace else," he stated suggestively.

"Everything is about to close, or at least stop serving alcohol."

"I've got alcohol at my place. Lots of alcohol, great foot rubs, and"—he grabbed his crotch—"a Mandingo dick that will put you to sleep like a baby."

I laughed. "Does that mean I'll be sucking my thumb after you lay it on me?"

"No, that means you'll be sucking my dick after I lay it on you. I'll be your pacifier."

A lot of women would have been turned off by Taariq's vulgarity, but with all the men who had paid me to fuck them, none of them talked dirty enough to me. I loved filthy mouths on men.

I got into my car. "I'll follow you. Where are you parked?"

Taariq pointed to an SUV. "I'm only five minutes away. Ten minutes from now, I'm going to be tearing that fine ass up."

"You talk a lot of shit," I said. "I only hope you can back it up."

"Baby girl, I hope you can back that ass up and make it bounce for Big Daddy."

Ten minutes later, Taariq and I consummated our relationship. We fucked and sucked until the sun came up and I claimed him as my man for all eternity.

Taariq immediately began to become suspicious about how I was spending my time. I worried that he could tell that I was fucking other people. They say a woman can tell when a man has been fucking around because of his ball sac being too empty or some foolish shit like that. I have seen a lot of balls in my day and you can't tell shit that way. Some men have a little bit of cum, some have a damn load, and some jack off so much that their balls damn near stay empty. Yet, I was still concerned that Taariq would somehow stick his dick in me one night and come to the conclusion that I was doing other dudes. That never happened, but the stress of the possibility almost killed me after three months of trying to live a double life.

Funny thing is that I had been living a double life for so long. Patience and Lyric had no idea that I was selling pussy to make ends meet. One day, over lunch, I let it slip out. Looking back, I realize it was intentional. I wanted them to know.

"I need to get ready to go," I said as we sat at the table finishing up dessert and drinking apple martinis. "I have a client coming over at nine and I need to have this pussy clean and fresh before he shows up. Raymond doesn't want to pay me if I'm not smelling like roses."

Okay, so it definitely was not a slip!

"Excuse me," Lyric said. "What did you say?"

Patience glared at me from across the table.

Lyric continued, "Did you say something about a client and having a clean pussy?"

Patience sighed. I did not respond.

Lyric gulped down the rest of her martini. "I must be in the twilight zone or some shit. I know you did not just say that."

Patience finally spoke. "I had no idea times were that hard, sis. Why didn't you come to me, Ana Marie?"

"Times have always been this hard," I said to Patience. "And what was I supposed to come to you and say? Hey, Patience, I'm having trouble making ends meet and I might need to start selling some ass to pay my bills?"

"That would have been a good start," she replied. "Then I could have kept you from doing it."

"Ana Marie, we've been friends since forever," Lyric jumped in. "Patience and I would never let you fall to the wayside."

I got loud on them. "I'm not a damn charity case! I'm doing what I have to do and don't you dare judge me!"

"We're not judging you, Ana Marie," Lyric said with sadness on her face. "We only want to help you."

"I mean, I didn't go to college like you two divas, and

comedy doesn't always mean a nightly gig." I went on the defensive. "Just because you two have great careers doesn't mean you have the right to down me."

"No one is downing you," Lyric said. "We just . . ."

Patience reached over and touched Lyric's hand. "Leave it alone, Lyric."

"But . . ."

"No, Ana Marie has instructed us to stay out her business and that is what we're going to do . . . for now."

I realized that Patience was dropping it only because we were in a public place. She has this way about her, and there was no way she was going to let it be with that. I went back to my place and "serviced" Raymond, got him out of there, and waited. Sure enough, come midnight, Patience was banging at my door.

"I'm not here to hold your hand, let you throw a guilt trip on me, and throw a pity party for you," were the first words out of Patience's mouth. "I'm here to set your ass straight."

She slammed my front door behind her, and that's exactly what she did. I have not turned a trick since, either. Patience made me a significant loan—one that we both knew I could never pay back—and she also told me that if I could not make it in comedy, she would hook me up with a job. That was out of the damn question.

Taariq and I moved in together shortly after the blowup with Patience. I have to admit that not having to worry about screwing men on the side is a relief, and with Taariq covering half the bills, things are going well. We have our ups and downs, two entertainers determined and struggling to become famous. Taariq is faring a little better than me, and his big break seems to be looming around the corner. A major producer caught wind of him, and they are in discussions of him cutting a CD. I am so happy for him. At the same time, I am not feeling the groupies that come along for the ride with musical stardom. Now, those are whores, straight up. While some have their shit together enough to hold out for some cash, most just want bragging rights on fucking someone famous. I see it all the time. Even when the famous male comedians come through the club, women are trying to make a beeline for their hotel rooms.

Taariq has no idea that I used to be a call girl. I will die if he ever finds out. Granted, he knows that I am not perfect, but he would never be able to accept my past. Men can fuck a thousand women, and I would not doubt that Taariq has fucked his fair share, but when a woman has been open about her sexuality, men condemn her worse than a serial killer. I want my relationship with Taariq to grow. One day, maybe we can even have a few kids and purchase a house in the suburbs with a wraparound porch. Who knows what will happen? But that is what makes life so damn interesting. We can all make plans, we can even make predictions, but our future is predestined. I cannot wait to see what will happen in mine.

Maricruz Aguilar

There are days you wish you could simply start over. Days you want to crawl back in bed, under the covers, and pretend like you never woke up. I have had a few days like that, but if I could take one day back and pretend as if it never happened at all, it would be the day that I caught Randall in bed with Stacy.

Randall had introduced me to Stacy before. I had walked into his office, to surprise him for lunch, and he said that she was a business associate in town from Dallas. I believed his bullshit hook, line, and sinker. In fact, I invited her over for dinner that evening because I felt sorry for a young woman alone in the city with nothing to do. She declined, stating that she and Randall had to work late since she was in town for less than twenty-four hours.

Like an idiot, I left, wishing them a wonderful lunch and productive day. Randall came home after three in the morning, stating that his brain was exhausted from so much concentration. I did not realize he was talking about the brain in his little head. Naïve me. I said something silly like, "Poor baby. Let me rub your feet for you."

I know, I know. I did not see the proverbial writing on the wall. It took catching them in the act to wake me up. It was a Wednesday. What they call "Hump Day" among federal government employees. Randall took that "hump" thing literally. Normally I would have been at work all day, but Flava had closed early because a water pipe burst and we were all sent home.

I decided to surprise Randall with a candlelight dinner, followed by a drawn bath and a night of intense lovemaking. I had plenty of time to make plans, and I was going to ask a neighbor to watch the boys so we could be alone. I went to the house first, to change into some casual clothes before I went to the grocery store. I parked in the driveway instead of the garage because I was going to be there only a hot minute. That's why I did not notice that Randall's Lexus was in its usual spot.

I did panic when I opened the front door and the alarm did not sound, alerting me to disarm it. I had been the last one to leave that morning but was sure that I had engaged it. I started to slowly back out the doorway so I could call 911 from my cell phone. That's when I heard it. That's when I heard that bitch scream out my husband's name.

When it comes to love, I have always been weak. I come from a very strict family where love is forever. Once you make a commitment to someone, that's it for life. A lot of my uncles have had problems: alcohol, drugs, but mostly women. None of my aunts have ever filed for divorce. They were taught to understand that a man will be a man, and I was raised the same way. As I stood frozen in the doorway, afraid to move, I weighed my options. There were only a few. I could go upstairs and confront them, curse them to high heaven, and tell Randall to pack his bags. I could go into the kitchen, find my biggest butcher knife, and send them both to the boneyard. Or I could pretend like it never happened and simply leave. What happened? I ended up waiting in my car, down the street, casing my own home to see who came out.

An hour later, Randall and his floozy pulled out of the garage. I recognized her immediately. Stacy from Dallas. They did not even try to hide their affection for one another. In fact, the reason they did not notice me is because she had her filthy tongue buried in his ear as they sped past me.

"I hope you crash into a fucking tree!" I yelled out after them. Then I started crying.

"What's going on, Maricruz?" Patience asked me as she answered her door. "Are you all right?"

I could not find any words. It was like my tongue had evaporated into thin air.

Patience guided me onto her living room sofa and sat beside me, placing her hand over mine. "What's wrong? Are the boys okay?"

"The boys!" I exclaimed, glancing at my watch. I was relieved to see that it was only a little past three. They went to aftercare until six, so I had some time.

Patience stared at me, her eyes full of compassion.

"They're fine," I said. "It's not about the boys. Then again . . ." I paused. "I guess this is really all about them."

"You are making zero sense, sis." She grasped my hand into a tight hold. "Calm down, take a deep breath, and tell me what is really going on."

I did as she instructed and sucked in air, held it for three seconds, and let it go. "Randall's having an affair. There, I said it."

"How do you know he's having an affair?"

Patience and I worked together at Flava Cosmetics, so she knew the office had shut down early. That's why she was at home, so I skipped that part of the story.

"I went home to change so that I could go shopping and plan a romantic meal for Randall. I was looking forward to following up the meal with my pussy on a platter. Silly me. He apparently got his eat on early, for lunch."

I could see the anger flash in Patience's eyes. She has this zero-bullshit-tolerance policy when it comes to men. "Are you telling me that that motherfucker had another woman in your bed?"

I did not respond, just stared at her.

"Is that what you're telling me, Maricruz? Don't let me find out that bastard did some shit like that to you."

Here it was that I had been cheated on and I was about to have to try to calm Patience down. She let go of my hand and started pacing the floor.

"So what happened? Did you kill him? Is his carcass still in the bed? Beside the whore's? Do we need to get rid of the bodies?"

"Patience, you know I could never do anything like that." I hesitated, then added, "But I did think about it for a hot second."

"Well, I guess you're right. He's not worth doing jail time for." She sighed. "What happened when you confronted him?"

I lowered my eyes to the floor.

"Sis, you did confront that low-down piece of shit, didn't you?"

"Um . . ."

"Um? Um, what?"

"Actually, when I came in the front door, I heard them upstairs. She screamed out his name and then I could hear the bed, *our* bed, squeaking and . . ."

"And you went up there and gave them both a piece of your mind, right?" Patience asked. "You kicked him out and told him never to show his face again, right? Maricruz? That's how it went down, right?"

"Not exactly," I whispered.

Patience put her hands on her hips and shook her head. I felt like such a coward.

"Okay, I know that I should have confronted them. I should have shown my ass six ways from Sunday, but I froze."

"You froze?"

"Patience, you know what kind of family I come from. I can't get a divorce. There are some things that a woman has to accept."

"Who made the rule that women have to accept anything? That's the problem these days. Women are too accepting and then wonder why they have jacked-up relationships." She plopped down in an armchair across from me. "You can't let this slide, sis. You've got to do something."

"I need Randall," I protested. "Outside of this, he's been a good husband. The boys need their father to—"

"To show them how to disrespect women by using you as a prime example?" Patience asked. "It's bad enough that he cheated on you, but in your own home? In your bed?"

I raised my voice. "I don't need you to remind me of what happened! I was there!"

"Oh, so you can confront me but you couldn't confront them?"

There we were, at a standstill, eyeing each other down. Patience spoke up first.

"I'm not trying to make you angry. I realize you're already upset. No one knows how much you love Randall more than I do, but love does not always have to mean pain." Patience paused. "Who is she? Did you recognize her voice . . . when she screamed out his name?"

"No, but I recognized her face when—"

"I thought you said you didn't confront them?"

"I didn't. I waited down the street in my car until they pulled out of the garage."

Patience smacked her lips and shook her head again. "So you sat out there and waited for them to finish fucking in your bed. How long did it take?"

"An hour."

"Damn! Randall can last like that?"

We both laughed, knowing that was not even the case. Randall was the love of my life and we had comfortable sex, but it was far from great sex. He was the only man I had ever been with, but even I knew that the biggest room in our house was the room for improvement.

"Who knows? Maybe she was in my house playing Suzy Homemaker and cooking for him."

"So who is she?"

"This woman named Stacy. She's from Dallas. A *business associate*. I met her awhile back in his office when I went over there to surprise him for lunch." I jumped up off the sofa. "This all makes sense now."

"What does?" Patience asked.

"He claimed they had to work late because I was going to invite her over to the house for dinner. What a fool I was. They both played me."

"You know that I'm pissed, right?"

"Yes, I know."

"You know that you have to take a stand, right?"

"I can't let go of my husband, like he's nothing. Like he's a pair of panty hose. He's my entire life."

"And what are you to him? An option?"

"That hurt, Patience."

"The truth always hurts, Maricruz."

Patience and I sat there and talked until it was time for me to pick up the boys from aftercare. Randall came home that night and, with the strength of the pep talk from Patience, I laid into him after the boys were soundly in bed.

Randall thought that I was kidding at first. Even though he knew that he had been busted, he could not fathom that I was actually demanding that he leave. He could not comprehend that I wanted a divorce. Instead of leaving, he took a shower and crawled into bed, telling me that we would talk more in the morning. The bastard did not even try to deny the affair. He seemed like he was proud of it. Nasty ass.

I called Patience at 1 A.M. and told her that Randall was refusing to leave and thought it was amusing. She said, "I'll be over there in the morning. Ask your neighbor to watch the boys."

I realized Patience meant business, so by the time she pulled into the driveway at 10 that Saturday morning, Mrs. Green had taken the boys with her to the football game at the local high school. Her oldest son was the quarterback. Randall was sitting at the kitchen table gulping down scrambled eggs and toast when I opened the front door for her.

As soon as she entered the kitchen, he said, "Don't even start. This is between Maricruz and me."

"Maricruz, why don't you go outside and get the newspaper. I saw it in the driveway," Patience said. She looked at me. "And take your time."

I did not say a word. I put on a jacket and went to get the paper. I sat on the front stoop and read the *World News*. I could hear them in the house screaming at one another. Less than fifteen minutes later, Randall was pulling out the garage.

"Maricruz, your friend is crazy!" he yelled at me. "If you want a divorce, so fucking be it!"

With that, he burned rubber as he screeched down the street.

Patience opened the front door.

"What on earth did you say to him?" I asked, getting up off the stoop and folding the paper.

"I made it clear to him that he had no choice but to leave. He's coming back to get his things tomorrow, with a sheriff." Patience reached out and rubbed my shoulder. "I'll be here when he comes . . . to make sure nothing gets set off."

A single tear fell from my right eye. "I don't know how I'm going to make it without him."

"You're going to take it one day at a time," Patience said. "Just like everyone else. Change is never easy, but you will get through this."

Patience asked Mrs. Green to keep the boys overnight so we could hang out with Eboni, Lyric, and Ana Marie. We went to the Black Screw, to see some male strippers. I felt uncomfortable, as usual. I had always believed that even looking at another man lustfully was cheating on Randall. Ana Marie, a real wild child, got up on the stage and rode the one they called "the Designer" because he was rumored to be able to redesign the insides of any woman he fucked to conform to his mastodonic dick. It is a good thing he had on underwear or Ana Marie might have stripped down her damn self and given him a run for his money.

I have never been a heavy drinker—really I am more of a nondrinker—but Lyric ordered shots for everyone. The clincher was that we had to do body shots off one of the strippers. I was likely to pee in my pants when it was my turn.

Patience leaned over and said, "Let Randall go. He is nothing but a liar. For the record, Stacy does not live in Dallas. She lives ten minutes from you, and he bragged about his daily booty calls while you were sitting at home with the boys."

I gawked at her. "What did you say?"

"Maricruz, Randall has been playing you for a fool all this time. Enjoy life. Don't let him steal all of your joy."

That made me angry. I did five body shots and then gave a stripper called "Judgment Day" a lap dance instead of the other way around. By the end of the night, I felt great. I felt liberated. I felt empowered. I felt like I could face the world . . . alone.

Randall did come the next day to get his things, with a sheriff in tow. Patience stood over me like a bodyguard and few words were exchanged. She took me to see a lawyer the following day, on Monday, and I began the divorce process. I was determined to start my life anew.

Okay, here comes the part that I hate to admit. Like I said, when it comes to love, I am weak. Even though Randall and I are divorced, I am still fucking him. Even though he lives with Stacy, I am still fucking him. Even though I know that I should have some self-respect, I am still fucking him.

For the past two years, Patience has tried to convince me that I need to stop letting Randall have the best of both worlds. Never in a million years could I have predicted that I would become my own husband's mistress. Yet that is exactly what I am, if you want to get technical.

My family has been of no help. They all think that I was a fool to get a divorced, that I was lucky if I knew of only a single affair when most men in our family were up in the double digits with theirs. What amazes me to this very day is how the women in my family act like it is a badge of honor to endure infidelity.

Here I am, divorced and sleeping with the only man that I have ever been with intimately. When I am out and about, especially at clubs with my friends, men try to come on to me. I do not even know how to receive the attention. Randall tells me that no other man will ever want me, being that I am so "inexperienced" and have "baggage." How can our children be baggage?

I will admit that he is a decent father. He loves our sons, and I only hope that they can somehow shift through all of the nonsense they witness and treat women better than their father has treated me. I heard that Stacy is trying to get pregnant. That sickens me. It also sickens me to know that we are sharing the same man . . . without protection.

Randall has respected me enough not to bring her around my house. He always comes alone to pick up the boys, but they often come home delighted with the "bribes" Stacy bestows upon them. Video games, sneakers, iPods, etc. I hate her and do not think it fair that she probably does not realize that we are man sharing. It hurts me to the bottom of my heart, but I am too embarrassed to confront her. What would I say? That the tides have turned and he now comes home to her every night and I am the sideline piece of ass?

This is it. This is the year—2008—that I will do what Patience is always telling me to do and "claim my pussy back." I am going to make myself the kind of woman a good man will desire. A man who knows how to respect and treat a woman. I will find him. I will stop sleeping with Randall. I will make my boys proud of me, and I will be proud of myself. Like Patience said, "Change is never easy!"

Hannah Bendenhall— "Eboni"

I was born in Little Rock, Arkansas, to two parents who were lost in time, way back in time. Daddy believed in two things while my siblings and I were growing up—work and church. Yes, family was a big part of his life as well, but we did not come before work and church. Daddy owns a sawmill, Bendenhall Mill, to be exact. It was started by my great-grandfather in the early 1900s. It has become a family tradition that all the Bendenhall men grow up to work in the mill. My three older brothers fell for that bullshit, and all three of them are married with kids and working ten hours a day in the mill. My oldest brother, David Bendenhall Jr., assumes that he will run everything once Daddy retires. Whenever he calls me to boast about it, I simply wish him the best of luck. He is going to need it because even though he is the oldest, Daddy favors Shawn, the youngest of the three, the most. Every day was "Shawn Day" in our house when we were young. "Shawn made straight A's again!" "Shawn learned how to ride the tractor!" "Shawn made the varsity basketball team!"

All of us had accomplishments as well. David Jr. was Student Body president, the captain of the football team, and could have gone to the University of Arkansas on scholarship. Instead, Daddy told him that all he needed to know was the sawmill business and convinced him to forgo college. David Jr. had a good chance of playing professional football but that was not in Daddy's plans. David is now married to Valerie—"a nice Jewish girl" according to Daddy—and they have three sons. I feel sorry for my nephews because they will certainly fall into the same mentality and live in Little Rock for all their days.

My middle brother, Hezekiah, was the brain in the family. He also made straight A's but never got the accolades like Shawn. I will give it to him. He did go to college at the University of Georgia and earned a business degree. I would have bet my bottom dollar that he would not come back and work in that mill. I would have been broke because he came back and handles all the books. He "counts the money," as Daddy says. Hezekiah is married to Tracy and they have a son and a daughter. Daddy does not like Tracy because she is not Jewish and is not submissive enough for him. He believes women should "submit and embrace order." I love Tracy and wish she could talk Hezekiah into relocating anyplace else but there. I feel like Hezekiah could be successful at anything he wanted to, if he would only get away from Daddy's clutches.

Shawn is the kisser-upper. Whatever Daddy wants from him, Daddy gets. I really do not have much more to say about Shawn except that he has a submissive wife named Carol and they have one son.

Yes, I do have a mother, and I love my mother more than anything in this world. Being the only daughter in the family, she and I spent day in and day out together waiting for the men to come home from work. Mom taught me how to cook, how to clean, how to sew, and just about everything else of domestic nature. It was expected that I would grow up, marry a man of their choosing, and settle down to birth babies. One could say that I am their biggest disappointment.

I loved getting an education and had a true thirst for learning. I did have a problem concentrating and was easily distracted, mostly by boys. I made decent grades but not good enough to get a scholarship. I applied for college in California, was accepted, and grew excited about escaping Little Rock. I will never forget the day that Daddy shot down that idea. My parents were sitting in the parlor when I rushed in with my acceptance letter from USC in my hand. I stood in front of the television, blocking their line of sight of the evening news, and read it out loud:

"Dear Hannah Bendenhall:

"We are pleased to inform you that your application for admission has been accepted. We look forward to you furthering your education at the University of Southern

California. Please contact the Admissions Department within ten days of receipt of this letter so that an admissions counselor can help you apply for financial aid and housing (if applicable) and make your registration process move along with ease.

> "Sincerely,
> Janet Allen
> Director, Admissions
> University of Southern California"

I glanced up from the letter and expected to see nothing but pride splashed across their faces. Mom looked like she had seen a ghost and Daddy had smoke coming out of his ears.

"Aren't you going to tell me congratulations?" I asked them.

Mom got up from her easy chair and headed to the kitchen. "I better go finish up dinner."

"Mom," I said to her back. "Mom, what's wrong?"

I later discovered that my mother had gone into the kitchen to weep.

I turned to Daddy. "Why are you looking at me like that?"

I should have never asked that question because the only thing that resulted from it was a hostile speech about how I was not going anywhere outside of Little Rock for the rest of my life. I ended up in my room, bawling my eyes out, but it was a revelation for me, Daddy's reaction to my college acceptance. By the time the sun rose the next morning, I had made a commitment to myself to get the hell out of Little Rock, Arkansas.

I never made it to college but I did make it to the big city. Even though I was the age of majority, my parents still called it "running away." They even filed a report. The police told them that I was not considered a runaway if I simply left. I did not disappear on them altogether but I refused to speak to Daddy for nearly three years. I would call the house, and if he answered instead of Mom, I would hang up. Mom and I seemingly became even closer after I moved. I felt "free to be me" and could discuss things with her without the fear of being treated like an outcast in their home.

Hezekiah and David Jr. even come to visit me from time to time. The first time they came to see me, I was residing in a studio apartment full of cockroaches and three pieces of furniture: a bed, a table, and a chair. I did not care, though. I was proud to have my own place and to be up from under Daddy's rule. My brothers, at least two of them, are happy for me. They only want me to be content. I was working as a waitress back then but had already decided what I wanted to do with my life. I wanted to own a spa named Steam and I wanted to make it the hottest thing in the entire city. I had all kinds of ideas and had visited some of the best around to see how I could enhance the already awesome experience they were offering.

It was at one such establishment—Dawn of a New Day—that I met Raphael. He was the hottest specimen of a man I had ever seen in my life. He was tall, bald-headed, built like a truck, and he was also African-American. Out of everything that Daddy griped the most about life in general, interracial dating was at least in the top three. None of us had ever considered it, if we wanted to continue breathing. But I was not in Little Rock, Daddy could not tell me what to do, and human beings are human beings. Thus, when Raphael asked me out, I accepted without the slightest hesitation.

Raphael was a marketing director for a clothing designer. He was such a sharp dresser that heads turned whenever we were out together. I do not know about him, but I quickly fell in love. He was definitely in lust, but I am not sure the love ever came. Sex with Raphael was almost scary, he turned me on so much. He took me places that I never imagined and damn near broke my back. He did not break my back, but he did break my heart into several pieces. As quickly as our relationship began, it ended when he decided that he wanted to get back with an ex-wife he had never mentioned.

I made a fool of myself the day I found out. I knew that Raphael was scheduled to attend an expo at the convention center. His company had a display booth. I showed up, paid the admission price, and hunted his ass down. I wanted to cause this big scene and tell the world what an asshole he was. I felt like he owed me at least that much.

I spotted him standing there, grinning like a cat, handing out circulars about their latest line. I marched right up to him and yelled, "You motherfucker! I hate you!"

Raphael looked like he had seen a ghost. "I don't know who the hell you are but you need to step off," he said.

He didn't know who I was!

"Raphael, I'm the woman you've been fucking for the past six months! Don't try to run a game on me!" I came back at him. "You never told me that you had an ex anything, rather less an ex-wife."

He tried to lower his voice and grab my elbow. "Hannah, you need to leave me alone, right now. Go home and I will call you later."

I knew that he was just trying to get rid of me. He thought that I was stupid enough to go home and wait for a call that would never come.

"I was good to you," I said. "You said that you would help me start Steam. We made plans."

"No, you made plans," he stated with disdain. "You made love, too. I was not even doing that. I was merely fucking you."

People were walking by, laughing. I am not sure what I expected. Empathy or compassion, maybe. They were shaking their heads, pointing and laughing. All except one beautiful African-American woman who was standing behind the table at the booth across from Raphael's. She looked like she wanted to beat the shit out of Raphael, and I wondered if she was also fucking him.

Raphael was still talking trash but I zoned him out. I was drawn to the woman's eyes, which met mine, and the expression in them transformed from anger to compassion. Yes, it was definitely compassion. She motioned for me with her finger to come over there. Somehow my feet moved without a connection to my brain and I ended up at the Flava Cosmetics booth, which is where I first met my best friend, Patience James.

"Would you like a free makeover?" she asked and handed me a pamphlet. "You have great skin."

"I . . . I . . ." I could not get the sentence out.

She looked in Raphael's direction. "Forget him. He is not worth it."

"Do you know Raphael?" I managed to ask.

"I don't need to know Raphael to get the picture. Girl, I know it's hard." She placed her hand on my shoulder. "These men today are a whole new breed. Most of them have zero respect for women and even less respect for themselves. The day they realize that a real man is not a man who has made love to a thousand different women but one who can make love to the same woman a thousand different ways will be a day to rejoice."

I laughed. I actually laughed, even though I should have been embarrassed and hiding my head in the sand. "Yeah, but will that day ever come?"

She shrugged. "The dinosaurs will probably have to re-inhabit the earth first, but we can always hold out hope."

"I'm so ashamed," I said, lowering my eyes. "He made a fool out of me."

"No, my sister, he made a fool out of himself. You need to lighten up. You had a pit bull in your bed and it's not a big deal. Ninety-nine percent of the women who try to put other women down because they got bamboozled by a dude have been cheated on themselves."

I guess that I was still naïve, coming from Little Rock and not having slept with a lot of men. "Damn, ninety-nine percent?" I asked.

"More like ninety-nine point nine percent," she responded. "This your first heartbreak?"

I nodded.

"Welcome to the club." She pointed to a stool. "Now, why don't you have a seat and let me make you look glamorous so you can go out tonight and meet your next pit."

We both laughed.

"I should go," I said, eyeing Raphael, who was standing at his booth staring.

"Look, forget that fool." She patted the stool. "Don't run because of him. He's not worth the aggravation, and if what he was giving you was a great dick down, those come a dime a dozen in this city." She extended her hand. "By the way, my name is Patience James."

I shook her hand. "Hannah. Hannah Bendenhall."

Patience made me over and I have never looked so good in my life. After she handed me the mirror and I saw myself, I grinned with pride.

"Wow," I said. "I hate to admit it, but when I saw Flava Cosmetics, I thought the makeup line was for women of color."

"We're all women of color," Patience said. "You've got color, my sister. Just not as much. In fact, if you told everyone your name was Eboni, no one would take a second glance."

"Yeah, right," I said and we both snickered. "Eboni, huh?"

"Yes, Eboni. In fact, let's go out and find us a couple of new pit bulls tonight, Eboni."

Patience and I have been the best of friends ever since. She introduced me to her two best friends from high school, Lyric and Ana Marie. She also introduced me to Maricruz, who works with her at Flava. I now have a group of friends outside of Little Rock and I love all of them for reasons as different as they all are. I took to the name Eboni even though Patience started it as a joke. Now I use it more than I use Hannah. It gets me instant attention and it is a great icebreaker at social gatherings.

Patience and I have been running through pit bulls together, but I move a whole lot faster than her. She is very cautious about whom she "allows to worship inside her temple," as she puts it, and I just love dick. At first, I was still falling in love with every man I fucked but realized sex does not equal love. Many women believe that once they give a man their pussy, the man will love and cherish them forever. They seem to forget the fact that all women have pussies and it is not the pussy that makes a man fall in love; it is everything else connected to the pussy.

One day I hope to find a man who wants to settle down and do right by me, but like Patience alluded to, the dinosaurs might actually have to reinhabit the earth first. Meanwhile, I will handle my business. Sex is a stress reliever for me, similar to shopping or playing Scrabble on the internet is for other women. Besides, I am around fine-ass men all day, my clients. Yes, I guess I should mention that.

Hezekiah convinced Daddy that he should loan me the money to start Steam, since there was zero chance of my ever returning to Arkansas. He told Daddy that it was a good way to get back into the good graces of his only baby girl. From what I heard, Mom actually cursed Daddy out when he first rejected the idea. In all my years, I have never heard Mom curse and would have loved to be a fly on the wall. Anyway, Daddy showed up one day at my waitress job, sat me down in a booth, and handed me a check for the amount Hezekiah had determined that I would need after he wrote a business plan for Steam. He told me that he loved me, wished me well, and asked me to stay in touch. He also insisted that I would let Hezekiah "count my money" to make sure that my business did not fail. That is exactly what I did, and now Steam is the hottest spa in the city. We have more than two thousand members, most of whom come through frequently. Out-of-town visitors make it a point to try to experience it. I truly am proud of myself, and in life, self-pride can go a long way.

Right now, I am seeing a few men, none of them ex-clusively. I am not a whore. Men see various women all the time to take care of their vast needs. I am simply doing the same thing. No man has put a ring on my finger and they make time for me when they want to make time. Why should I be sitting by the phone waiting all the other nights? It is not fair and I wish more women would stop sitting around trying to be faithful to men who are not thinking about being faithful to them. As for me, Eboni is going to live her life while Eboni still has a life to live.

Lyric Stansfield

"It's cold out here. Don't catch pneumonia."

I recognized the voice immediately. Estaban Cruz had been my biggest crush all through my residency at Metropolitan Hospital. He was the head doctor on call, and every time the residents had to follow him around from patient room to patient room, I was in heat.

"Oh, I'll be okay," I said, turning around to face him on the front steps of the hospital. "My ride should be here any minute."

He lit up a cigarette and that was a slight turnoff. I have never understood how doctors—out of all people—could smoke. When I was in college, I worked in a kidney dialysis center part-time to make ends meet. The employees and even some of the patients would gather in the smoking station outside the front door and puff like there was no tomorrow.

I decided to speak my mind. "Why do you smoke? I've been meaning to ask you that for a while." He pouted and I felt ashamed for asking. "I'm not trying to get in your business or anything."

"Then why did you ask?" he stated sarcastically.

"Okay, so I am trying to get in your business a little."

He glared at me and then laughed. I snickered and rubbed my hands together. It was freezing out there, even for a February evening. Rodney was late picking me up again. He was probably with that ex-stripper-hooker-tramp-slut of his. Rodney had played out, but I was still seeing him only because I feared being alone. He had absolutely nothing going for him, but his bedroom skills were hard to beat.

Estaban, on the other hand, had a lot in common with me, starting with the fact that we both look at coochies for a living. Yes, we are ob-gyns. I became a gynecologist because, from an early age, I was fascinated with the miracle of life. My mother gave birth to my younger brother while we were in my daddy's pickup truck, stuck on the side of the highway in the middle of an ice storm. We had been visiting my maternal grandparents in Connecticut, against Daddy's objection. He said it was a bad idea but Mommy would not hear of it. She insisted that we visit her parents for Christmas. On the way back, all hell broke lose and she gave birth a month early. I was seven at the time, and the events that took place in that truck had a major impact on me. I wanted to be able to bring new life into the world. That feeling never left me. When my high school guidance counselor asked me what my chosen profession was, I quickly told him that I wanted to be an obstetrician. I attended the University of Connecticut for undergrad so that I could spend some time with my elderly grandparents. They have both since passed on, but I enjoyed my time with them and resided in their home for the entire four years, instead of getting a dormitory room.

I moved back after college and went to a local medical school. I missed my friends, especially Ana Marie and Patience. Four years of separation—even with holiday visits—was hard on me. Since high school, we had been like one. A lot of things happened while I was gone, as I later found out. Everything is back on the right path now, and we hang out often, along with Eboni and Maricruz.

Anyway, back to Estaban. He kept me company while I waited another twenty minutes for Rodney, who pulled a no-show and would not answer his cell. Estaban offered me a ride back to my apartment and I accepted. On the way, he asked if I was hungry, and even though I was far from famished, I started rubbing my stomach like I was. If I could have made it growl on command, it would have been a perfect acting performance.

He took me to a nice steakhouse, and what I expected to be a casual meal turned into something spectacular with porterhouse steaks, champagne, and sharing six-layer chocolate cake for dessert. Those two hours in that restaurant changed my life forever. Estaban was a recent divorcé with two practically grown children. He had married his ex-wife right out of college, and while he seemed to respect her, he thought that they had compatibility issues. I loved the fact that Estaban did not attempt to trash his ex-wife. So many people, on both sides of the sexes, do that in order to make themselves feel good. I remember when a friend of mine from medical school was dating this man who claimed his ex-girlfriend—the mother of his child—was spawned from the devil. He said that she was making him pay a ton of child support, which was why he could not afford to take my friend out a lot, and that she was a horrible mother. One day, when my friend was visiting his family, she started trashing the woman in front of them. His sister set her straight, drove her to the woman's home, and my friend felt like a complete idiot. The woman was brilliant, beautiful, obviously a very loving and nurturing mother, and she had not received a dime in child support in two years. I do not know why people are so quick to believe bullshit.

Estaban actually appreciated the years that his ex had devoted to him and to developing his children he was so proud of. He harbored no ill feelings and hoped that she would one day find another man to love and cherish her. As he related all of this to me, instead of the normal "my ex is a crazy bipolar bitch," I grew to admire him more than I did already. That night he dropped me off and left me with a handshake, but we both knew that there was an interest on both sides.

I decided that I would not pursue him. I wanted to make sure that he wanted more than a "friends with ben-efits" situation and that he was comfortable with our age difference. He would mention it often, the age difference. I would always reply with the same answer, that I adored the fact that he was mature and past the stage of playing games. Do not get me wrong; I am not a fool. There are still plenty of men in their seventies running game, but some do learn from their past mistakes and grow. I sensed that with Estaban.

We took our time. It took us nearly two years to make a commitment to one another. I did not want to rush because even though he seemingly had come to terms with his divorce, they were together a long time and he stood the chance of wanting to go back. Ultimately he chose me. The night he proposed was unforgettable.

We were in Paris, on vacation. I had always wanted to visit there, but that was my first time leaving the United States. Estaban booked us a suite for one week at the Hôtel Ritz Paris on Place Vendôme. It was a breathtakingly beautiful mixture of rare wood, silks, and brocades, with Carrara marble in the luxury bathroom. Estaban and I had incredible sex in that suite. I wanted to rip it out and bring it back with us. Our suite overlooked the rooftops of Paris and the Opéra Garnier. The Ritz has an average staff of three people per guest at your beck and call, so the service was impeccable. While we did dine out a lot and in L'Espadon—their main restaurant—we also took advantage of their room service and woke up each morning to homemade brioches and breakfast pastries.

We took in as many tour attractions as possible. We made

love the first night there, and on day two, we went to see the Eiffel Tower and Musée Marmottan, where more than sixty-five paintings by Claude Monet are exhibited. On the third day, we went to Luxembourg Gardens and La Madeleine, a beautiful church built by Napoleon in honor of his troops. The fourth day we went to the Louvre and Notre-Dame. The fifth day we went on a bike tour that was inconceivable fun but also told me that I needed to hit the gym more. We must have biked fifty miles, but Estaban barely broke a sweat. On the sixth day, we decided to lie up in our room all day before we had to head back to the hustle and bustle of our city life in the States.

After a serious lovemaking round on our last night, I decided to take a quick shower to get ready to blow Estaban's mind some more—both of his minds, the one above and the one below his waistline. I was lathering up with my favorite bath gel, when Estaban suddenly yanked the curtain back. For a second, I almost slipped. He had never gazed at me like that before. At first I did not recognize what I saw, but then it dawned on me. Estaban was in love with me, really, really in love. The kind of love that I had searched and hoped for my entire life.

"You scared me," I blurted out, meaning it in more ways than one. *Could I actually handle that kind of emotion?*

"Why are you scared? You knew I was in the room," he said, then chuckled.

"I know. It's just that . . . You've never looked at me like that before."

"That's because I've never felt this way before."

Damn, I was psychic that night!

"Do you love me, Lyric?" he asked, standing there in a bathrobe while I was covered with lather.

"Yes. I love you, Estaban."

"We've been together for a while now, right," he stated.

"Two years and counting," I said. "It's been a great two years."

He unfastened the robe, dropped it to the floor, and climbed in the shower with me. "I stand here before you, Lyric, in all of my naturalness, with all of my soul, to profess my undying love and affection for you."

I felt tears gathering in my eyes. "That's so sweet."

"It's sweet, but do you believe me?" Estaban asked.

"Why wouldn't I believe you?"

He sighed. "I realize that a lot of men in your life have hurt you, have lied and disappointed you. I also realize that I come to the table with one failed marriage on my record, but that was truly a matter of incompatibility and growing apart. I never cheated on her or disrespected her and . . ."

"Estaban, you don't need to validate what happened in your divorce to me. I accepted you as you came to me, and I wanted to be with you before that night you offered me a ride. Long before."

"Really?" He blushed. "I never knew."

"Well, you were married, so you weren't supposed to know." I rubbed my fingertips across his hairy chest. "You did not seem like the type to step out on your marriage and I'm definitely not the type to sleep with a married man. That was not our time. Now is our time."

"Yes, it is." He took my hand and kissed it. "That's one of the reasons that I wanted you to see Paris. I want you to see a lot of the world and I want you to see it with me."

"I'm not going anywhere, Estaban." I pointed to my heart. "You're in here and I can't let that go."

"What do you think about starting a practice together?" he asked, which threw me off-kilter from our present discussion.

I shrugged, then said, "We've discussed it before. I love the idea, but do you think you can handle working with me and being with me every night?"

Estaban and I were not living together but we might as well have been. Either he was over my place every night or I was at his.

"Sure, I can handle it but . . ."

"But what?"

"There's only one stipulation."

I frowned. "A stipulation?"

He reached down for the robe and pulled out a velvet box. I gasped and threw my hand over my mouth. "Oh, no!"

"I hope that's not your answer, before I even open up this box." Estaban flipped the lid open. "Lyric, my stipulation is that when we start a practice together, we do it as husband and wife. Will you do me the honor of becoming my wife?"

"Yes! Oh, yes! I will!" I exclaimed, throwing my arms around his neck and planting kisses all over his lips and face. "I will marry you!"

Estaban placed the four-carat emerald-cut diamond

with a platinum band on my hand. "Then you're mine, for-ever!"

"I only hope forever is a very long time!" I said and then commenced to blowing his mind, both of them.

The sex between Estaban and me was incredible . . . before we tied the knot in a wedding that cost upward of twenty thousand dollars. We made love every night and practically every morning. After we started our practice, things began to change. Part of me believes it is because he views me as a competitor, which is silly. We are in this together and I am merely trying to pull my weight to make the practice successful. Naturally there are some women who feel more comfortable with a female obstetrician. Then there are those who do not want another woman anywhere near their pussies. In our case, the number of women who pre-fer a female doctor is slightly higher. At times, we will see each other's patients, but most do have a preference and set their appointment accordingly. This is no different from any other practice, whether it is pediatrics, neurology, or endocrinology; everyone is entitled to choose. Personally I am elated that business is booming. Even in a big city we have to hold our own with all the other doctors around. Those other doctors are Estaban's competitors, not me. Yet, sometimes I feel myself going on the defensive when he makes certain comments.

The other thing that changed after our marriage was his relationship with his ex. Estaban tried to remain friendly and cordial, but obviously she did not expect or want him ever to fall in love again. She took it as an insult to her womanhood and began to start a bunch of bullshit when it came to Estaban's relationship with his children, and her financial demands doubled after he married me. She figured that if he could afford a wife, he could afford more support for their offspring. Most of that money is going toward sustaining her lifestyle and not for their kids. Some men are truly paying child support, but a lot of them are paying ex-woman support. Even as a female, I can admit that.

Estaban and I fight a lot now. Not physically, because my baby would never go there. The stress of us working together, the stress of his ex and her drama, and the stress of life in general have put a strain on us. I know that he loves me, never doubted it for a second. He has become withdrawn in many ways, though. There was a time when I could wink at him and he was jumping my bones. Now I can be butt-naked and he is acting like he doesn't even know that I exist. I did not marry Estaban to have someone to fuck. I could fuck fifty times a day and not be married to anyone. I married Estaban for companionship, and being able to make love to him is important to me. I need him. He is like my medicine.

I have discussed this with my friends, but they have their own issues. Ana Marie is trying to get Taariq to make a commitment but, at the same time, she does not want to come clean to him about her past. Maricruz is trying to get over her "dick addiction" to her ex-husband Randall, a no-good bastard who is shacking with the woman he cheated on Maricruz with but still makes booty calls over her crib.

Eboni is doing her thing, searching for love in all the wrong places but not understanding that she needs to take a breather from seeing a few men at a time so Mr. Right does not have to fight through a sea of dicks to get to her. As for Patience, she has this zero-bullshit-tolerance policy when it comes to men. That should be her middle name: Patience Zero-Bullshit James. Sometimes I feel like she will never settle down as long as she keeps dismissing men from her life the second they do something she deems uncouth. All of them view me as the lucky one. Since I am the only married one, does that necessarily make me lucky? There are a lot of people in miserable marriages, and the divorce rate is at an all-time high.

I should not even mention the word "divorce." I would never do that to Estaban. Whatever our problems, we will work them out. I have to rekindle the flames, that's all. All of this drama will eventually blow over. He will realize that having me as a partner—both in and out of the office— is a blessing and not a curse. He will learn to ignore that bullshit from his ex and deal with it until his kids come of age and can make their own decisions. He will stop tripping over little things that mean nothing, and we will get back to making love like we used to. I realize that over time, and because of our age difference, his dick will ultimately shut down. That's okay. I look forward to polishing his rocking chair and even changing his diapers. I love him that much and I know that he loves me back. He loves me so much that he stopped smoking. Now that's what you call "pussy power"!

To all the women in the world——young, middle-aged, and elderly——who still feel we were placed on this earth to service men. May Zane's Sex Chronicles liberate your pussies, free your minds from the chains of sexual oppression, and make you realize that you are entitled to fuck your way.

Damn, Sex While You Wash Your Drawers?

I was planning to stay home that night because I was pissed the hell off about my breakup with Trevor. I had to go out, though, and it wasn't like I was going clubbing or any shit like that. I was simply going to the coin laundry to wash some damn drawers. You know how it is when your panty supply gets down to the wire. When you are single, working twelve hours a day, and living without the convenience of a washer and dryer up in the crib, you wait till the last minute and take about five baskets of clothes to the 'mat at one time.

That is what I was doing that night—getting my wardrobe straightened out. When I got to the 'mat, there was no one there except this one sistah with the most hardheaded set of twin boys I had ever seen in my life. How she managed to fold clothes and stay calm enough not to beat some ass was beyond me.

She was piling the kids and the laundry baskets of clean clothes into her minivan when he pulled up in a Mazda RX-7. I was sitting there chillin', reading an issue of *Essence* that was about fifty fucking years old I found in the torn-up and ragged collection of mags on the antique table in between the only two pleather chairs in the joint, when he got out of his ride.

My first instinct was, *playa*. Shit, aren't they all? My second instinct was, *foine*. The bruh made my one pair of previously fresh drawers, the ones I was wearing, instantly wet. Made my juices get to flowing. Know what I mean?

He started bringing his clothes in, and he was a typical bachelor. He had his shit in plastic trash bags and had one of those miniature boxes of laundry powder he probably paid too damn much for at the convenience store down the block.

"How you doing?" He gave me a holla while I was sitting there enjoying the view, a Coke, and a smile.

"Fine, and you?"

My southern drawl seemed to be ten times more profound than usual, and that shit only happens when I am horny. Trevor used to always laugh at my ass because I would start talking like a country bumpkin every time he started hitting it from the back.

He divided his clothes like a good little Boy Scout, separating the colors and then tossing them into three different washers.

One of the four dryers my clothes were occupying went off, and I got up to retrieve a rolling cart to move the clothes from the dryer to a laundry table.

He spoke to me again. "So, what's your name?"

I was not even trying to hear it. Foine or not, I was sick-da-hell of men and had sworn off the dick for at least three months. "I don't have a name."

He smirked at me. "Yeah, right!"

"You, bruh-man, are a stranger, and my momma told me never to talk to strangers."

I couldn't help but giggle as I said the shit, because I was sounding more like a four-year-old than a grown-ass woman.

"Hmmm, yeah! You better watch out for me. Late at night. Empty Laundromat. Full moon!" We both laughed.

"Your ass is silly!"

I got my clothes over to the table and started folding them up. I was getting kind of "shamed" when I noticed him watching me separate my bras from my panties and socks.

"Need some help?" He was looking my ass up and down like a bear eyeing a pot of honey. "I don't have shit to do at the moment but wait for my clothes to wash."

"Now why would I want your crusty hands all over my drawers? No telling where those things have been."

He walked closer to me, and my pussy started throbbing. Why, I have no clue, but my pussy lips were jumping like two castanets. "You are too cute. Tell me your name."

"Hells naw! I am not telling you my name, and you sure as hell better not tell me yours, because I could care less."

"Really?"

He was standing so close to me by that time, I could feel his breath on my neck, and it smelled like peppermint. Fresh breath has always been a turn-on to me. That au naturel shit has to go.

"Yes, really."

I started folding my shit faster because my black lace panties were getting soaked, and I knew pussy juice would start trickling down the inside of my legs any second if I didn't get the foine-ass nucca the hell away from me.

I don't know what the telling signs were, but he knew I wanted his ass. He decided to go for it, and men who are sexually aggressive make my toes curl. I hate the nuccas who look dumbfounded when you tell them to pop a tit in their mouth or suck on your pussy. Some men can't deal with uninhibited sistahs.

He was not fronting, though, and my ass cheeks started throbbing when he brushed his dick up against me. He was about five inches taller than me, so his dick was pressing up against the small of my back. Felt damn good, too. Of course, I was not about to tell him that.

"What the hell do you think you are doing?"

"Helping you with your laundry."

"Bullshit!"

He reached around me, with one arm on each side, and started folding up my panties. I froze. "You know, you forgot a pair?"

"Huh?" I was lost like a virgin in a whorehouse.

"You forgot to wash a pair of your panties."

"Bruh, you trippin'. How you know my panty count and shit?" I turned my head toward him and looked up at him.

"You forgot to wash the pair you have on. Let me help you take them off."

He strategically moved his hands from the laundry table to my breasts and started palming them bad boys. Perfect fit, I might add. Like a hand to a glove. Then came the tricky part. I stood there debating whether I should stay on my dick starvation diet and push his hands away or give in to my desires and enjoy the ride.

I looked out onto the street in front of the Laundromat, and there was not a soul in sight. There we were, exposed because the entire front of the place was glass. At that moment, something popped into my head. I decided it was time to stop "freaming" and start "freaking." For those of you who don't know, "freaming" is dreaming of doing freaky shit your ass would never have the nerve to do while you are awake. I pondered over it and decided it was time to get jiggy with it.

I looked at him. He looked at me. I whispered, "Fuck the bullshit!" and it was on. We started tonguing the hell out each other, and he had a thick tongue. Just the way I like them, especially when the tongue is licking my other pair of lips.

I caressed the back of his neck with one hand and his juicy ass with the other as we kissed. His kisses reminded me of the first time I ever kissed a boy back in junior high school. They were passionate and yet a bit rushed.

He turned me around slowly by my hips as our tongues

continued to intertwine. Then he started caressing my nipples, which were now very erect and protruding through the sheer material of my spaghetti-strap sundress. That was the moment I knew I was going to fuck that man every which way from Sunday, public place or not.

He reached underneath my dress, and I gratefully spread my legs so he could get two fingers into the elastic of my black lace panties and into the sanctuary of my wet, pulsating pussy.

His fingers felt like they were performing a sensual dance on my clit, and my juices started accumulating.

"Let's take these off." I didn't argue with his suggestion and even helped him along. After they were completely off, he lifted them up to his mouth and sucked my pussy juice off the crotch. Damn, I was just *too* through.

With my panties still in his mouth, he picked me up and sat my ass on top of one of the washing machines that was on the rinse cycle. It was there that he fucked my ass royally.

He ripped his dick out of his pants so fast that I didn't even see him unfasten them. Then he took a condom out of his pocket, ripped it open with his teeth, and snatched it out the package. I wanted to laugh because he was trying to seem intimidating, and the shit was not even working.

"You think you can handle all this dick?"

I glanced down at it. It was *huge,* but I wasn't about to give him the satisfaction of letting him know I was truly impressed. "It is rather large, but I've seen *and had* bigger dicks than that inside me."

He winced at my comment and jimmied the condom onto his dick. It barely fit, and I began to get a bit nervous. "Well, you may have had bigger dicks, but you've never had any man fuck you as hard as I'm about to fuck you right now."

"Humph, promises, promises."

He rammed his dick in me and ran his thick tongue up my neck. "How's this for promises?"

"It's a start," I barely managed to say—his dick inside me took my breath away.

The vibrations from the machine added to the experience, because it felt like someone was fondling my ass at the same time.

He went fast at first and then slowed down, gazing in my eyes and planting small kisses on my chin. "Admit it," he said about three minutes into the act.

"Admit what?"

"That this is some good-ass dick." I didn't say a word, so he started going in and out so fast that my inner thighs started trembling. "Now admit it."

I still would not say the words he wanted, so he took his dick out, pulled me down off the machine, and turned me around. My stomach hit the cold surface of the machine, and he kneeled down, spread my ass cheeks open, and started licking the crease of my ass.

"Ooh, you're so nasty!" I exclaimed, loving every second of it.

"You're right." He slapped me hard on the ass. "Now admit you haven't had a man like me before."

I smirked and then lied. "I've had plenty."

He stood back up and then stuck the tip of his dick on my anus. "You talk a bunch of shit. I wonder what you'll say if I stick this all in you."

"I'll say the same thing I just said. That I've had plenty."

"Then get ready to say it," he stated with disdain before sticking it all in me at once.

"Oh, shit!" I yelled out in pleasure.

He pumped his dick around in my ass until he came a few minutes later.

"So what do you have to say now?" he asked as he de-flated inside of me.

I gulped before answering, "Okay, I admit it. You have some good-ass dick."

We both broke out in laughter and fell to the floor just as the washer went off.

I never saw the bruh again. Although it wouldn't have been such a bad thing. It just wasn't in the cards, but at least for one night I actually did something totally off the chain. I was telling my best friend about it the following weekend, and once I finished relating the story, she looked at me in amazement and exclaimed, "Damn, girl! Sex while you wash your drawers? You're my damn shero!"

The Airport

You meet me at the airport right on time after my return flight from Jamaica. Even though I had a great time vacationing with my friends, I can hardly wait to see you. My eyes light up as I see you walking toward the gate to meet me. You look so sexy in the khaki slacks, black jacket, and white button-down cotton shirt. I can feel my panties begin to get damp underneath the red spaghetti-strap sundress that I have on.

I look into your eyes and see the same sparkle that is in my own as you put your arms around me. Just then, a female customs agent approaches me and says she needs to search my bags. She is very pretty in her regulation uniform and has long dark brown hair, hazel eyes, and smooth caramel skin just like mine. She searches my bags and then tells me she needs me to follow her to a room.

I grow concerned because I have no idea what she thinks I am guilty of. I follow her to a nearby room while you wait for me by the gate. She takes me in the room and tells me she needs me to disrobe so that she can strip-search me. I ask why, and she says it is common procedure, with women traveling alone from the islands, to ensure I am not smuggling drugs in as a mule.

I obey and take off my dress. I am braless, and all that remains on are my red silk panties and my black high-heeled shoes. She instructs me to take my panties off as well. She approaches me and lifts up each of my breasts, examining them, and I begin to realize what it is she really wants. She tells me to turn around and bend over the single table in the room, and I comply. I feel her spread my ass cheeks open, and then, without warning, she sticks a finger up my ass. I immediately get nervous because I have never been with a woman before. Yet her hands on me, and now her finger in my ass, are making me very aroused.

I can see her take a seat in a chair at the end of the table out the corner of my eye. Then she sticks her tongue into my asshole, and I shiver. While I know that you are waiting patiently for me to come back out to the gate, I begin to wonder how far she is going to take this.

I don't have to wonder long, because she tells me to turn around and face her. As soon as I do, she cups one of my breasts in her hand and begins suckling on my nipple, more gently but with more intensity than any man ever has.

Suddenly I hear the door creak open, and you are standing there. You have a look of shock mixed with excitement on your face as you close the door, asking, "What the hell is going on?" She looks at you and tells you, "Just watch and see!"

My ass is resting on the edge of the table as she lifts one of my legs up over her shoulder and begins sucking on my clit with a hunger I have never known. You can feel your dick come to attention because this has always been a fantasy of yours we have talked about but I swore I would never do. She sucks on my pussy for what seems like an eternity until you decide you cannot take it anymore. You are about to bust.

You tell her to move out the way so you can taste my sweet pussy too, now dripping wet from all the attention it has been given. She gets up from the chair so you can sit down, and you push me all the way onto the table, forcing me to cross my legs behind your shoulders as you begin to devour my clit.

She watches for a few seconds and decides she will not be left out, so she bends over and begins sucking on my breasts again. I caress the back of your neck and run my fingers through her hair with my hands. Her ass is protruding up in the air, and you reach underneath the skirt of her uniform and start finger-fucking her while she continues to suckle on my nipples. I can feel your tongue deep inside my throbbing pussy.

I tell you to get undressed, you do, and then I let you take my place on the table, laying you down on your back with only your feet hanging over the edge. I sit on your face while she begins to suck your dick, deep-throating it without any hesitation. I am facing her, hands caressing your chest, watching her partake of your dick as you partake of my pussy and finger-fuck my ass.

She comes up for air, and I bend over to take over, sucking the head of your dick to get some of the precum out because I remember how delicious you taste. I contract my cheek muscles tightly around the head, trying to get every possible drop I can. She is licking up and down the shaft of your dick and sucking on your balls while I continue to work on the head.

We both begin sucking and licking your dick. We are so hungry for you. I can feel cum trickling out of my pussy as you lap it all up off my thighs. Saliva starts to escape the sides of our mouths as we take turns deep-throating your dick.

We can hear planes landing and taking off and people walking by in the hall, but none of us gives a damn, 'cause this is just too good to let go. Other than that, there are just a bunch of sucking noises and the delightful smell of sex in the air. The aroma is breathtaking.

As you suck on my clit even harder now, fingering my ass with one hand and palming an ass cheek with the other, I take my tongue and lick your belly button, then blow on it to make it dry before I wet it again with my tongue. I know how much that turns you on. I continue to do this for a couple of minutes while she deep-throats your dick.

I slowly take my pussy off your face and slide my wet pussy down over your chest, then your belly button. I tell her to let go of your dick so I can straddle it. I sit on your dick, facing away from you so she can suck on my breasts while I ride your dick. I can feel the head of your dick begin to part my pussy lips as you pump your hips up to meet my downstrokes. You are still finger-fucking my ass, but with two fingers now.

I move up and down on the shaft of your dick while she flickers her tongue at my nipples. You marvel at how tight my pussy is. I take a little bit more of it in each time I go up and down until it is all in. As I begin to grind my pussy onto your dick, she pushes both my tits together and suckles on both nipples at the same time.

Your back is arched off the table, meeting my every thrust as I start to ride your dick faster. I take my long tongue and flicker it over one of my nipples while she sucks furiously on the other one. My pussy is so hot and tight, and you try to pump and reach the bottom of it harder and faster. I put my hands on your thighs so I can get better leverage, and I begin to go up and down on your dick faster each time. You admire my ass, with your fingers in it, as it goes up and down. It looks so juicy.

Contracting my pussy muscles on your dick, I squeeze it hard as she gets the chair and sits down in front of us and begins to suck on my pussy and lick your dick while I am riding it, tasting us both at the same time. She reaches up and rubs my nipples while she is sucking on us both. I continue to fuck you hard, and I can feel my cum trickling down the inside of my thighs, down between your thighs, and onto the tabletop.

You take your other hand and pull me back by my hair

so that I am lying with my back on top of your chest, still riding your dick. You start palming my breasts while she continues to get her eat on, and we are all moaning. My pussy juice is everywhere. I want you to shoot your hot cum all down my throat, and I ask you, "Will you cum for me?" and she says, "I want some of it, too!" You tell me, "Whatever you want, I will do." So I get off your dick, and she and I both wait anxiously for you to give it to us. Your dick is throbbing, and veins are popping out of it everywhere. You look so yummy.

We both get on our knees as you stand up. We begin licking and sucking all over your dick. You stand, your knees feeling a little wobbly, and hang on to the side of the table. I take the base of your dick in my hand and begin to squeeze it gently. You grab both of our heads and begin pumping your dick into our mouths fast and furiously. As I take your balls into my mouth and bounce them on my tongue, you tell us, "I'm about to cum!" We can hardly wait. It starts to shoot out, and we both take some of it with our tongues and place some on our fingertips, rubbing it all over each other's breasts and faces, both of us smiling with delight. I whisper, "Hmmm, you taste so good, boo."

I get greedy, and I take your whole dick into my mouth, trying to get every last drop and contracting my cheek muscles around your dick, making all of it come out into my mouth as I arch my neck so your dick can hit my tonsils. You tremble as the last of it goes down my throat, but I continue to suck 'cause I want to get you hard again so you can fuck me in the ass before we leave. I tell you, "I want you to take all this ass right here!" She interjects and says, "We have to finish up before someone gets suspicious."

We all laugh as we get dressed. She finishes first and gives us both a smooch on the lips before she leaves, saying, "Thanks for the afternoon snack!" We leave and go to the baggage claim, where my bags have been spinning around on the belt for the last half hour or so. We go out to the car and you seat me in it while you put my baggage into the trunk. I sit in the car, waiting for you patiently, fingering my own pussy and then sucking my juices off my fingers. My pussy is so wet. After you get in and proceed to the exit gate, I take my free hand and rub it up and down your thigh, then to your crotch, and start to undo your zipper.

You reach in the backseat and hand me the card and box of chocolate-covered cherries you bought for me because you missed me so much. After we clear the exit gate, I continue to caress your dick and balls with one hand as you finger my pussy. I put one of my feet up on the dashboard so that my leg is up in the air and you can get to my pussy better. I roll down the window so that the cool breeze can blow through my hair and hit up against my legs and pussy as we hit the highway.

I want you to fuck me again, but I know I have to wait until we get home, or at least until we get off the highway, because I know how you like to make sudden stops. I decide to open the box of cherries instead, and one at a time, I put them in my pussy, drowning them with my juices, and then begin feeding them to you with my fingers. Needless to say, we pull off at the first rest area we come to. And there, on the hood of your car, you give me what I crave and fuck me in my ass just the way I love it.

The Headhunter

Let me tell you straight up that my situation will seem crazy to the average person. But, for me, sex is an incredible way to make a living. The simple version of the story is that I make money, a *whole lot* of money, doing what most women have been doing for free since the beginning of time. I have sex for money. No, I don't mean that I'm a hooker. Hell, no. I don't stand on anyone's corner waiting for Lawd knows who to stop his car and offer to take me to an alley for some quick, cheesy sex. Nope, not me. In fact, while I sleep only with men, 100 percent of my income comes from women. *Successful women.*

It's like this. A lot of women these days are extremely busy building their careers, making their dreams come true, etc. They don't have the time or the patience to hang out in nightclubs, churches, or wherever else, trying to find a decent man. That's where I come in. I locate and "test out" brothas for sistahs that want to get to the crème de la crème without all the hassle of trial and error.

I have an ad that I run in the local weekly paper. I haven't changed a word of my ad for the past five years, because it works like a charm. Like they always say, "If it ain't broke, don't fix it." My ad reads:

Looking for a good man?
Let Vixen Headhunters, Inc.
Find the perfect man for you
Whether you like them big and tall
Or short and small
We will locate your perfect mate
Call 301-555-HEAD
For a confidential interview

Vixen Headhunters is my brainchild. I started out running this gig alone, but now I have six full-time employees. My name is Gypsy, and hell no, that's not my real name, but it is the name I go by. In case the law ever comes sniffing around, I am not about to have my real name mixed up in jack shit. In fact, that is a requirement for all of my employees. They can't give out their real names to people because in the end, that's only asking for trouble—especially if one of the brothas we "test out" becomes overly infatuated with the sex or even worse, pussy-whipped. None of us want to be bothered with that bullshit. Our work is all about the benjamins. Dick is dick. There is nothing special about any one in particular.

Now there have been a few men who stood out from the rest. Not because of their actual dicks but because of their other amenities. For instance, there was this chick named Linda, a stockbroker from a rich background that had afforded her a lot of financial opportunities, but not a single freaky one. She wanted to meet a man who was successful enough for her to take home to her parents. She was desperate enough to look over the fact that she was butt-ass ugly, though heavily endowed.

This was a tough assignment for the team, because none of us are even close to butt-ass ugly. We're all fine as shit. But Linda was paying me a grip, so I told the other girls I would handle it. I went to see an image consultant—not to look better, but rather to look worse. I asked Harold—a transsexual who looked more like a woman than half the women I'd seen—to transform me into something hideous. I wanted him to make me look fucked da hell up, and that's exactly what he did.

He put some kind of gook on my long, ebony hair that made it mat up something crazy. Then he removed my fake nails and trimmed my real ones down so low that they looked like I had been biting them daily since childhood. He gave me these drops that made my eyes turn red and some fake teeth that protruded about an inch from my regular ones, giving an entire new meaning to being buck-toothed. He also gave me this pencil to use to make these nasty-ass blackheads all over my face.

Then came the hardest part of all: wearing off-the-rack clothing. That was the most traumatic experience of my entire life. I can't understand how sistahs can play themselves by stepping out the house in any outfit that costs less than three bills. I'm designer all the way. I mean, come on, we only live once.

I made sure that no one I knew saw me walking into a department store, one of those ones where you can purchase everything from laundry detergent to screwdrivers to toilet tissue to *clothing*. Cheap-ass clothing. I found this little cotton dress that wasn't even twenty bucks and a pair of ten-dollar shoes. Yuck!

I tested the waters that night at this club where all the big ballers supposedly hung out. Not! It was a teeny-bopper club, and none of the men in there could have been making more than thirty grand a year, unless they were slanging dope. Linda wouldn't be able to present a drug dealer to the family, so they were out. A lot of the men and women snickered at me, and I don't blame them. I did look busted. However, there was this one chick gritting on me that I almost had to set straight. I started to tell her that I pull down more ends in one night than she probably made in a damn year.

I tried again the next night but scoped out a jazz club instead. Now we were talking. Most of the men in there were coupled off, but there were a few lingering around the bar who were obviously flowing alone. One in particular stood out from the rest; he looked like money, and he was fine.

I made my way over to the bar and asked if the seat next to him was taken. He assured me that it wasn't, and I sat down. It was time to go to work. His name was Kincaid, he'd never been married, wasn't seriously involved, and made about half a million a year. Yes, he would do.

Kincaid did seem a bit apprehensive about talking to me at first, but after a while, I guess he figured that any attention from a woman was better than none. I told him my name was Sheila, not that I consider Sheilas to be busted, because I know a few fly-ass chicks with the name—it was just the luck of the draw and the first name that came to mind. We chatted throughout the evening, and then I came on with it. He was obviously qualified in the basic departments and had not cringed at my face, so the only thing left to find out was if he could fuck.

The club had last call and people were getting up to beat the bum rush to the door. I leaned in to him, caressed his wrists, and asked, "So, you want to go someplace and do me?"

"Do you?" he asked with a raised brow, playing dumb.

"Yes, do me. You know, fuck me. Cum inside me. Hit it from the front and the back. Make my toes curl. All that." I flicked my tongue over his outer ear. "I bet I can make your toes curl."

He grinned and searched the room, probably to see if anyone was looking at my ugly ass pressed all up on him. "I don't believe I've ever had my toes curl."

"Then you've been missing out."

He took my hand and got up. "Where do you want to go?"

I did not hesitate. "Your place."

Going to his place was a must. I had to make sure his ass

was not lying about his financials. More important, I needed to assure that his ass was indeed single in every sense of the word. Men tend to have various definitions of single, and I wanted to find out if Kincaid's was the right one.

We went back to his place, and it was exquisite. He had mad taste. It was actually a town house, but shit, the thing had to run about eight hundred grand, and the property in that particular neighborhood was appreciating with lightning speed.

As soon as we got inside, I started taking off my clothes. His chin almost dropped to the floor. While I looked busted in the face and had skanky hair, there was nothing I could possibly do to mask my bomb-ass body. He was impressed.

"Um, would you like something to drink, Sheila?" he asked after composing himself.

"Yes, I want some dick milk." I went over to him and stood before him naked. "So take off your clothes."

"You don't want to talk first?"

"We talked at the club. I want to fuck."

Kincaid took his time undressing, and it was all I could do not to yawn. Once I finally saw what he was working with, I was a little disappointed. He wasn't tiny, but he wasn't a Mandingo either. That wasn't my problem, though, because I was getting paid to check out the dick, not marry it.

I pushed him down on the sofa and climbed on it by straddling my feet beside his thighs. I lowered my pussy onto his face and demanded, "Taste me."

At first, I thought he was going to punk out and push

me away. Most men can't handle aggressive women, but Kincaid fooled me. He lapped at my pussy like it was a bowl of milk and then pulled me down harder onto his face. His tongue slipped inside my pussy walls, and it was nice and warm and thick.

I put my knees up on the back of the sofa so I could balance myself better. I moved my pussy back and forth on his tongue and palmed my breasts with my hands. Kincaid grabbed a handful of ass with each hand and started nibbling on my clit.

I sat on his face for a good thirty minutes and came to the conclusion that Kincaid was definitely a prize catch. This was before I had actually experienced the dick. Any man that could eat pussy like that was worth coming home to every night. There are some men who do it just to satisfy the woman, and then there are those who do it because they love the way it tastes. Kincaid undoubtedly loved it.

Once I climbed off his face, I fell back on the sofa in exhaustion. That didn't last long because Kincaid got on his knees between my legs and lifted my ass up until it was elevated to his dick. He entered me and worked it like a pro. My shoulders and head were the only things touching the sofa. Everything else was elevated. This was definitely a new position for me. I was used to being multiorgasmic, but damn, I came so many times that I lost count.

Kincaid and I went at it for at least four hours before falling asleep on the dining room table, another place where he had made me cum half a dozen times. I crept out of his place before he woke up, walked down to the corner, and caught a cab back to the club to get my car.

I reported to the client the next day that I had found the perfect mate for her, and she had a courier bring my final payment over in cash. Cash is always the way to go in this business.

Less than six months later, I saw their wedding announcement in the paper. I couldn't help but yell out, "You go, girl!"

Linda was a lucky sister. I knew that firsthand. There have been a few others like Kincaid, but they are few and far between. Business is booming these days now that the word has really gotten out. I am considering taking on some more girls, but there is such a thing as growing a business too fast, and the more girls, the more the risk that someone will run their mouths and end up getting us all locked up.

For now, I'm going to continue to do this business, because there is nothing like searching for "good head."

A Flash Fantasy

When I arrived at the building in the warehouse district, I was a bit apprehensive. Not because of the neighborhood. It had character—the kind of character it takes generations to acquire.

I was on pins and needles because I hate to have my picture taken. I've been that way ever since childhood. When I was seven, I was a flower girl in my cousin's wedding. I refused to take pictures with the rest of the wedding party. She had to chase me around the churchyard in her bridal gown for ten minutes before she persuaded me to cooperate.

I scanned the nameplates beside the column of doorbells until I spotted the one with "Curtis Givens—Photographer" engraved on it. I hesitated before pushing the little black button. I had to go through with it. It wasn't like I had a choice. My boss demanded I get a professional picture taken for the new corporate brochure he was having printed up for all of our clients.

When the intercom squeaked, it startled me. "Who is it?" a deep, baritone voice inquired.

"Evoni Price from the Grayson Corporation," I replied hesitantly.

The only response was the loud buzzer, letting me know I was free to enter the building.

I took the freight elevator up to the third floor. Before I could lift the gate, a strong muscular hand did the honors. I glanced up into the sexiest damn, brownest damn, most enticing damn eyes I had ever seen.

"Welcome to Givens Photography Studio," he said, grinning at me and revealing a cinematic smile. "Come on in and make yourself at home."

I followed him into his domain. I purposely trailed a few steps behind so I could get an eagle's-eye glimpse of his perfectly formed behind.

He directed me to a black leather love seat. "Please, have a seat, Miss Price. Or is it Mrs.?"

"No, it's definitely Miss," I replied, not sure why I was stressing the point. Maybe it had something to do with the fine specimen of a man standing before me.

He was just the right height, the color of bubbling brown sugar, and he looked twice as sweet. I had the sudden urge to lick him like a lollipop to see if it gave me a sugar rush.

"Would you like a mug of coffee before we get started with the shoot?"

"No, thanks!" Lawd knows, I was nervous enough without caffeine intervening. I was about to get my picture taken, I hadn't been laid since I was promoted to Vice President of Promotions, and a sexy-ass man was within striking distance to me.

"Maybe some water or a soft drink?"

"No thanks, I'm fine. Really!"

"Indeed, you are!" Our eyes met again. My knee took on a life of its own. It started rocking back and forth, causing a friction on my clit. "If I had known such an attractive sistah would be showing up on my doorstep this morning, I would've dressed for the occasion."

"You look just fine." Hell, he looked better than fine. He looked like a glass of ice-cold water in the middle of the desert; mouthwatering. He was wearing a pair of drawstring navy cotton pants and a white body-hugging T-shirt that revealed every ripple and muscle of his toned physique.

"Well, I'm going to grab some coffee if you don't mind. I'm still feeling a little sheepish this morning. I tend to be a night owl."

"Nothing wrong with that," I commented. "I work very long hours myself."

"I hope you're not all work and no play. A young, vivacious sistah like yourself needs to paint the town every now and then."

"I wish. The only painting I get to do is touching up my nails."

We shared a laugh, and he headed off to the kitchen. I

couldn't help but notice the size of his feet. Umph, umph, umph! Let's just say my peter heater went up about fifty degrees.

While he was gone, I took a quick survey of his place. It was a huge apartment with a loft. I immediately wondered what type of bed he had stowed away. He looked like a waterbed man to me. I was willing to bet he could make a lot of waves.

There were photographs hanging all over the walls of beautiful African-Americans: men, women, and children. I was thoroughly impressed. The walls were an eggshell hue, and they worked wonderfully in contrast to the colorful pictures. The flooring was wooden parquet, and he had expensive throw rugs scattered here and there.

His voice in my ear startled me because I didn't hear him come back in the room, much less walk up so close to me that I could feel his breath on the nape of my neck. "Shall we get started?"

"Fine by me," I mumbled, not looking forward to posing for a camera. "Where would you like me to sit?"

He surveyed the room while he sipped on his java and then pointed to one of the windows with his free hand. "I think over by that window would be great. The sunlight hitting up against your beautiful skin would be perfect."

I tried to control the blush, but it simply wasn't happening. I looked into his mesmerizing eyes. "You really think I have beautiful skin?"

He quickly responded, "I think you have beautiful everything!"

We stared at each other, and I suddenly had the urge to jump his bones. He finally broke the trance and cleared his throat before taking another swig out of his mug. He put the coffee down on an end table and then moved a crate over by the window. I watched him intensely while he covered it with a black velvet blanket. Then he held out his hand for me.

I walked over to him. The moment I took his hand, a surge of electricity shot through my entire body. I wondered if he felt it, too.

"Why don't you have a seat right here?"

"Thanks!"

He positioned my shoulders and held my chin up until he was satisfied with the pose. "Hold it right there. Don't move."

He quickly retrieved a camera with a long lens and squatted down a few feet in front of me. "Smile for me, beautiful."

I couldn't do it. I couldn't smile. I was suddenly encased by fear. I started gnawing on my bottom lip and my hands began trembling uncontrollably.

"What's wrong, Evoni?"

I looked into Curtis's eyes, but no answer would come to my lips. Instead, tears came to my eyes.

"I'm so ashamed!" I jumped up from the crate, wiping my eyes with the sleeve of my suit. "Look, this just isn't a good day for me. Is it all right if I schedule another appointment? Maybe for next week sometime?"

I was headed to the door, after retrieving my purse and

keys off his sofa, when he grabbed me by the hand and swung me around. "What's wrong with you, Evoni?" he reiterated. "Have I done something to upset you?"

"No, it's not you!" I exclaimed. The last thing I wanted him to think was that he had offended me. "I know that this is silly, but—"

"But what?"

He looked so sincere, so comforting, so sexy. "I hate having my picture taken."

He started laughing something terrible. "Is that all?" I lowered my eyes to the floor. "A lot of people get nervous about having their picture taken. Just relax."

He let go of my hand and started caressing my shoulders. It felt so damn good. I still wasn't relaxed enough to pose for a picture, though. I had no idea what I was going to tell my boss. I would just have to make up something. The brochure would have to go out to our clients minus my picture.

I pulled away from his embrace. "I'm sorry. I just can't do this. You've been so kind to me. I'll definitely recommend you to all of my friends. Do you have some extra business cards I can hand out?"

There was an uncomfortable silence for a few minutes. I could sense his eyes all over me, exploring my face, my body. Then it came out of nowhere. *The kiss.*

He took my face in his hands and lifted it until I was lost in his eyes again. He started with my forehead. Short, sweet, tender kisses. His lips moved down to the ridge of my nose and glided down slowly and methodically until they found mine. My mouth gratefully and hungrily accepted his tongue without hesitation. Before I knew it, I was totally engrossed in his arms and he in mine.

Our kisses became deeper. The next thing I knew he had me up against the wall with my legs straddled around his waist, and my blazer was toppling to the floor. Then the kisses stopped as suddenly as they began.

He put me back down on the floor gently and took my hand. "Follow me."

I whispered, "I would follow you anywhere."

He led me into the bathroom and then shut the door. I assumed he wanted to take a shower or bath together. Much to my surprise, he twirled me around until we were both facing a full-length mirror on the back of the door.

"Why don't you like to take pictures, Evoni?" He reached around me and started unbuttoning my blouse. "You're so incredibly beautiful."

I stood there, frozen, and glared in the mirror while he seductively removed all of my clothing, nibbling on my neck and shoulder blades while he went about his task. Once I was entirely nude, he took my pert breasts into his palms and rubbed my hard nipples between his thumbs and forefingers.

One of his hands dropped down and found the cherry between my thighs. I was in a trance, somewhere between reality and heaven's gate. His fingers worked magic on my clit and explored my pussy lips with a tenderness I had never felt.

Then he blurted it out. "Let me take your picture. Let me take a picture of the *real* you."

I was still nervous, but by that point, I was so much into him that even taking a picture was acceptable. Posing in the nude was something I never imagined doing. Hell, I never even wanted to pose with clothes on, but for this man who went by the name of Curtis, I was not only willing but eager to please him.

"Okay," I replied, taking a hold of the hand between my legs and guiding his fingers deeper into me. I stared at him in the mirror. "Take my picture."

We left the bathroom, and he laid me down on his waterbed. It was covered with red satin sheets. He removed the pins from my hair, letting my hair flow down around my shoulders. He bent over and kissed me. "Wait right here, baby."

He left to get his camera, and while he was gone, I played with my nipples. I had never masturbated in front of a man before, but I didn't stop when he reentered the room. In fact, I put on a show for him.

I masturbated while he took pictures of me. I can't believe I can actually just come out and say it like that, but that's exactly what I did and I have no regrets. I didn't look at the camera, though. I shut my eyes and pretended it was his hands on my breasts and fingering my pussy. I imagined him taking me right there on his bed, grabbing my full hips and pulling them deeper onto his dick, partaking of me from the front and then from the back. I imagined him suckling on my nipples and nibbling on my ass cheeks. I imagined him sliding his dick in and out of my mouth, and his cum trickling out of the sides and down my chin, splattering on my breasts. Then, when I had imagined it all, I came all over his red satin sheets. I came in front of the camera. I came like I never had.

He snapped one last picture, and then I heard the humming while the camera automatically rewound the film. It was that moment I opened my eyes. I was shocked to see that he was naked. To this day, I still don't know when he took off his clothes. All I know is that he looked good. Damn good.

I sat up on the bed and reached out my arms for him. He put the camera down on the foot of the bed and joined me. Then I jumped his bones for real. We did all the things I had imagined when I was masturbating.

Curtis and I have been living together for more than a year now. Our wedding is next month. I just can't wait to see how the wedding pictures turn out.

Lust in a Bus Depot

"Simone? Is that you?"

I turned around to see who was calling out my name. "Wendell? Wow! Long time, no see!"

It had indeed been a long time since Wendell and I had laid eyes on each other—at least four or five years. We walked up to each other and engaged in a long, comforting embrace.

"Damn, Simone, you look fantastic! How long has it been?" His smile was still the same. So beautiful, I wanted to jump his bones.

"Hmmm, it has been quite some time. Funny how time flies." I was in shock, but tried not to show it. Ever since my freshman year in high school, I had wanted Wendell. I was always too shy to tell him, though. I spent hours upon hours daydreaming about him in class, but he never knew it. He was so busy dating all the cheerleaders and school queens, I'm not sure he even cared.

In high school, I was dumpy and far from a sex goddess. My mother used to imply that I purposely made myself look unattractive so boys wouldn't pay me any mind. Looking back on it, I realize she may have not only hit the nail on the head but all the way through the fucking headboard.

I got lost in thought, daydreaming again, when the woman over the loudspeaker started blaring out the bus arrival and departure schedule again. Her voice was nothing short of obnoxious and knocked me out of my trance. Wendell wasn't saying anything either. He was too busy checking my new and improved ass out.

The Simone from high school and the Simone standing before him in the bus depot were from two different planets. I was shy all the way through high school, but everything changed when I got to college. Two people are responsible for the dramatic changes in me that came about freshman year: my roommate and my man.

Melinda was my roommate freshman year and was a real wild chile. She insisted I shed the dumpy look and threw hoochie clothes on me instead, did my hair and makeup, and even showed me how to seduce a man. At first, I thought she was plum foolish, but after being bored to death too many weekends in a row while she was out on dates, I decided to give it a shot.

It didn't take long for the Melinda Mind-Bender Plan, as she called it, to work. I met Duncan at the very first club we hit on my virgin voyage into the nightlife. The areas Melinda couldn't help me in, Duncan damn sure did. He taught me how to free myself from the imprisonment I created in my mind growing up. He taught me how to experiment with my feelings and emotions, wants and desires. In other words, he taught me how to fuck.

Duncan used to get this pussy anywhere and everywhere and at anytime. I never complained. I was glad I had waited for the right lover to come along because he broke my ass in right. I never loved him, though; never that. It was almost like fucking a play brother or something. I cared for him, but not in a relationship kind of way.

Eventually my feelings, or lack thereof, caused our demise. That was perfectly cool with me. It's not like I was sweating it or anything. I left the relationship with more than I entered it with, and that's all that matters.

Wendell, on the other hand, is a different matter altogether. I always wanted the real deal with him. Now that fate had intervened, I wasn't about to let the opportunity slip by to get with him. "So, Wendell, what are you doing in a bus depot in Charlotte in the middle of the night?"

He laughed. "I might ask you the same thing. I'm on my way from NYC to Atlanta, and you?"

"Oh, you still live in the Apple, huh? I live in D.C. now. I'm on my way to meet my parents in Florida for a few days. Gonna do the mouse-ears thing." We both giggled like a couple of kindergarten students.

"How long before your bus leaves?"

"Hmm, about an hour or so, but you know how it is with buses. An hour could mean three."

People were walking past and bumping into us, since

we were in the direct path of the main pedestrian traffic inside the terminal. Wendell suggested we find a couple of seats and helped me with my duffel bag. The bag was extremely heavy, and it was a relief not to have to drag it for a moment. As usual, I had packed everything but the kitchen sink and would end up not wearing even half of the clothes in it.

Wendell and I sat there, reminiscing about the good old days for about half an hour. Underneath my calm and cool exterior, I was working myself up into a frenzy. My eyes kept wandering to the gigantic clock on the depot wall, and I was dreading the moment when we would have to split up again.

What if I didn't see him for another four or five years? Ten years? Ever again? The mental anguish was too much to bear. Even though there had been drastic changes in my personality since high school, in an instant, I reverted back to those days and was shy all over again.

The time Wendell and I had together was seeping away like sand in an hourglass. I couldn't imagine not knowing how good the sex between him and me really would be. So I went for it! Wendell was talking about the weather when I blurted it out. "Wendell, how about a quickie?"

"Wha-wha-what you mean?" He started stuttering.

"How about you and I going somewhere right quick and fucking the shit out each other?" I looked him dead in the eyes so he would realize I wasn't kidding.

"Let me get this straight, Simone!" He started blushing. "You want to fuck me? Right here? Right now?"

"Word!" I put my hand on his knee and started caressing his thigh. "So where do you suggest? We don't have that much time."

"Ummm, let's see!" Wendell started looking around the depot for a suitable spot, as did I.

As an afterthought, I asked him, "Do you have a condom?"

He looked at me with that damn-I-can't-get-none look on his face and replied, "Naw, boo, you?"

"Nope! Where there's a will, there's a way, though." I jumped to my feet and told him, "You look for a spot, and I'll be right back!"

The little convenience store inside the depot had closed at midnight, so I was shit out of luck on that end. I was about to go tell Wendell maybe we could hook up some other time when I spotted what I was looking for. Standing over in a corner were three guys in army uniforms. I knew one of them, if not all of them, was packing a condom, so I simply went over, tapped one of them on the shoulder, pulled him aside, and asked, "Got a condom?" He was a bit surprised, since he probably was expecting me to ask the time or to bum a cigarette, and wanted to know if he was going to get the privilege of using it on me. I told him, "No, not tonight." He and I both laughed while he gave me one from his wallet.

I went back to look for Wendell. Our bags were there, but he was nowhere in sight. I heard someone whistle and turned around. I spotted him by the ladies' bathroom area and rushed over to him. We only had about twenty minutes left before my bus was due in. That was the one and only time I was hoping to have a transportation delay.

Once I entered the enclave, I noticed there were two separate ladies' bathrooms, each with its own door. The only other things in the enclave were a row of three pay telephones and a cleaning cart containing a mop, broom, cleaning supplies, rolls of toilet tissue, and packages of paper towels.

Wendell asked me to go into the one on the right and see if it was empty. I went in and checked to see if all the stalls were vacant. One wasn't, but I heard the toilet flush. I went back out and told Wendell it should be empty in a moment, and it was. An elderly woman, who appeared very down on her luck, exited the bathroom and walked away.

Wendell grabbed the CLOSED FOR CLEANING sign off the side of the cleaning cart, which I didn't even notice at first, and put it on the door. We rushed inside, and I sat on the countertop area, where there were about five or six sinks lined up along a huge mirror.

"Are you sure you want to do this, Simone?" I was hoping his ass wasn't having second thoughts, worried about being faithful to some lover he had waiting for him back in NYC.

"I've never been more sure about anything in my entire life!" I motioned for him to come over to me, opened my arms, and said, "Come here, baby!"

If he did have any reservations, they didn't show any longer, because he hurried over. I wrapped my arms around his neck and my legs behind his back. We started kissing and taking off each other's clothes.

We didn't take off everything. There wasn't enough time. He pushed my coat off my shoulders, and it landed sprawled out on the countertop. I lifted my shirt and bra so he could get to my nipples. He pushed my panties to the side.

While I was lying back, with the rear of my head pressed against the glass of the mirror and Wendell sucking on my nipples, I ripped open the condom packet with my teeth and pulled it out, tossing the wrapper into one of the sinks.

I undid the zipper on his jeans and whipped his dick out. I was overanxious, we both were, but I was determined to get some of his dick before I got on any damn bus. I told him to let up off my tits for a minute so I could slap the condom on. I had a little trouble getting it on 'cause his dick was so thick. We really needed one of those extra-large condoms, but beggars can't be choosers.

After managing to get the condom halfway up the shaft of his juicy dick, I made a special request. "Now, boo, fuck me like this is the last pussy you'll ever get!"

Wendell must have taken the shit to heart because he rammed his dick up in me and tore my little pussy up. I pressed his head between my breasts and worked my pussy all over his dick.

I heard a little girl outside the rest room door and told Wendell to stop for a second. He raised his head up, stopped pumping his dick into me, and we both listened intently. The only sounds were water dripping from a couple of the faucets and our heavy panting.

"Mommy, over here!" The door to the bathroom started opening, and I was thinking, "Oh, shit, no! Don't let that little girl come in here!"

As if someone was answering my prayers, I heard her mother say, "No, Lisa, that one's closed. We have to go in the other one."

We were both relieved and went back to fucking. Wendell started fucking me so hard, my head was banging against the mirror. I was getting one hell of a headache, so he told me to get up and bend over the counter. No sooner had I assumed the position before he was at it again. As usual, being fucked doggy-style made me cum something fierce.

Just then, the obnoxious-sounding woman on the loud-speaker announced my bus was now boarding. All I could say was, "Shit, not now!"

Wendell was about to take his dick out, but I told him not to. "No, boo, I want you to cum too. Just fuck me faster until you do!"

That's when I had to control myself from having spasms and shit. Never had I been fucked so royally. For it to finally happen in the bathroom of a bus depot was a trip. He fucked the hell out of me, and I know I came at least three more times in the few minutes that followed. Wendell finally came and pulled it out real quick when they announced the final call for my bus.

I pulled my shirt and bra down and flung my coat over my arm while Wendell got himself together real quick, ripping the condom off and making a nothing-but-net shot into the trash receptacle.

We rushed out the bathroom, and I noticed there was now a little crowd of people outside the enclave area. I really didn't give a fuck, though, because I got mine. Wendell grabbed my duffel bag from the seating area and hurried behind me outside to the bus loading area. I located the bus that had a sign for Orlando, handed the driver my ticket while Wendell flung my bag underneath the bus in the luggage area, and then got on.

I didn't have a pen on me anywhere and asked the driver for one so I could scribble my number on the envelope my ticket had been in. I wrote it down, handed it to Wendell, gave him a long wet kiss, and told him I would be home on Monday.

As the bus was pulling away, I waved at Wendell and drew a heart with my finger in the dew that had gathered on the cold window. I fell asleep before the bus made it thrity miles from the depot. I dreamt about him and woke up with his scent all over me. I could still feel his saliva on my lips and breasts.

I got home the following Monday afternoon, and Wendell called me that evening while I was doing the dinner dishes. I was thrilled, because I wasn't sure he would call. We talked for hours on end, and he told me how he wanted to get with me all through high school as well, but didn't know how to approach me.

Wendell and I spend at least one weekend together a month now, sometimes more. He and I catch the bus back and forth from D.C. to NYC to see each other. Every time we pass a bathroom in the bus depot of either station, we remember the time we did the wild thing in Charlotte. I told Wendell one day I want us to take a long cross-country train trip and get a private compartment so we can fuck in about ten states all in one shot. His reply was, "Hell, boo, why not?"

Nymph

My name is Page, and I'm a nymphomaniac, a sexual thrill-seeker, a sexual renegade. I love playing with fire, living a life full of drama and excitement, defying all the good girl rules, approaching situations that are both sexy and perilous. I'm a sexual rebel, and to me, danger itself is the most tremendous sexual stimulant of all.

One night I was at a club, and this sorry excuse for a man asked me was I pure. I asked him, "Do you mean pure as in pure chewing satisfaction?" He was dumbfounded, so I added, "Unless you want to suck on this pussy tonight, get the fuck!"

Like most men, he was intimidated by the sexual prowess I exude. Men like him disgust me. They brag about how they're all that in bed and can make a woman scream out their name when half the time they have trouble even finding the clit. As for the G-spot, forget about it. They couldn't find a woman's G-spot if she handed him written instructions and a map.

Fortunately for me, there are plenty of mad fuckers around, too. A mad fucker is a man who doesn't talk about turning a sistah out. He just does it. A mad fucker is a man whose cum tastes so damn good, it makes a sistah feel drunk. A mad fucker is someone who fucks a sistah so hard, the next day her pussy and nipples are sore, she has a helluva stomachache, and she has trouble sitting down. That's how you know you've been the victim of a mad fucker drive-by.

Sex to a nymphomaniac is like doughnuts to a police officer. We both gotta have it. My body is so accustomed to cumming, if I don't have at least three orgasms a day, I feel sick. Sometimes when there's no man around, which is extremely rare because I have more male bitches than the electric company has switches, I make myself cum through the art of masturbation.

Masturbation is damn sure an art, too. Everyone can't do that shit like a master. Those of us who have surpassed the amateurs masturbate so well, sometimes it seems like we're actually fucking. I often wonder why people feel it's more kosher and acceptable to touch the private parts of someone else than their own. Silly as shit, if you ask me. If you don't want to play with your own coochie-coo, why should a man?

I play my whole body like it's a trivia game. What's the strongest part of a woman's body? Her tongue. What are the most sensitive parts of a woman's body? Her tits and clit. Where does a woman like a man to insert a finger during sex? In her ass. What's a woman's favorite sexual position? Doggy-style. What parts of a woman's body should be sucked and licked on during foreplay? All of them bad boys.

When it comes to sucking dick, move over, 'cause there's a new sheriff in town. I can just picture a big juicy dick in front of my face right now. Slobbering all over it, making those slurping sounds, teasing it around the tip just before I deep-throat the whole thing, bouncing my head up and down as I catch a good rhythm, licking and gently sucking on the nut sac, swallowing every last drop of cum. Ummm, damn, makes my pussy ache just thinking about it.

There have been several mad fuckers in my life, starting way back in high school with Ryan. I remember one Thanksgiving, he invited me over his parents' house for dinner. After dinner was over, everyone except the two of us went downstairs to the family room to watch a football game.

Ryan and I were supposed to be cleaning off the table and washing the dishes, but we got sidetracked. Ryan took me off guard by forcing me up onto the dining room table and sitting in the chair between my legs. He pushed my panties to the side and starting fucking me with a roasted turkey leg. After he fucked me with it, he ate it down to the bone.

Ordinarily, the notion of being screwed with a greasy-ass turkey leg would be unappealing to me, but the fact his family was just a split-level away cheering for their respective football teams to win turned my ass on. That was the first sign I was kind of out there.

Then I started a scrapbook in high school where I kept everything from nude photos of myself and some of my menz to a male pubic hair collection. I even had a collection of used condoms with the guys' names written beside them in the book. My friends thought I was a true freak, and they were right.

There were other signs as well, omens so to speak, of what I would be like as I got older. I used to wear teddies under jackets to school with no shirt and flash the boys. My sex education teacher made me go to the principal's office for bringing a small vial of Ryan's sperm to class as a visual aid for my project on the reproductive system.

I was so desperate to go to a sold-out Prince concert one time that I bet these two guys I could sit on their dicks without making a noise in exchange for a pair of tickets. I couldn't sit on their dicks without making that dick-slapping-against-the-pussy-walls noise, but I fucked them both big-time and they gave up the tickets anyway.

Yeah, I was a bit out there in high school, but that's what growing up is all about. My senior year in high school was the year I discovered watching others having sex was just as big, if not bigger, a turn-on as doing the nasty myself. I'm quite the voyeur.

Camcorders were not popular back in the day. When I couldn't actually witness the act, I would ask my gurls to audiotape their sexual escapades for me so I could cop a listen. My gurls were wild also, but nowhere near as off da hook as me.

Four of us had a female singing group. We called ourselves Rough, Ready, Sexy, and Steady. We used to prance around in my gurl Winnie's living room after school in lingerie, singing everything from Teena Marie to Vanity 6.

When I got to college, my sexual rebellion really took off. Freshman year, I joined the sweetheart court for one of the fraternities on campus. Once again, another year brought with it yet another revelation. My freshman year, I discovered I like trains, and I don't mean Amtrak. The only thing better than one good dick is ten good dicks. The more the merrier!

I used to have men wait in my gurl Cherise's dorm room, down the hall from mine, until it was their turn. One day I had so many men waiting to hit this, some had to wait out in the hall. Hell, I even had my manager from the fast-food restaurant, a married man, up in that bitch. It's all good, though. Oftentimes, married dick is the best dick of all.

Don't turn your nose up at me because I fuck other women's husbands. I never took vows with and promised to love, honor, and respect no damn body. I can tell you this much. I'm the woman your mother warned you about. Don't let me in your house, because if he's fine, I *will* take your man. If I borrow a pair of shoes, your best bet is to make me throw them bad boys out the window of my car at 50 mph, 'cause if you let me in, I'm leaving with more than some 9 West pumps. And don't let your man have some of that turn-your-ass-out-Alabama-blacksnake-make-a-pussy-scream-out-his-daddy's-name-dick. Forget about it! I'm going to fuck his ass every day, married or not. Well, at least I'm honest. Most women will just go behind your back and do it. I'm telling you my plans straight up.

Am I a freak? Hell, yeah! Do I care what you think about me? Hell, no! You can kiss my black ass. As long as there's a breath in my body and I can spread my legs, I'm gonna get some dick.

My favorite mad fucker of all time was Sutton. Sutton was this dude I met at the house party of all mutha-fuckin' house parties. A friend of mine, Faye, was house-sitting for a wealthy couple in the upper-crust part of town. The house was the bomb. It had eight bedrooms, a circular living room, and a full staff of servants. It also had both indoor and outdoor swimming pools.

There were a good hundred people at the bash Faye threw, the food was slamming, and the bars were stocked with enough liquor to fuck everyone up. I had on a black hoochie dress covering up my black thong bikini. Yes, I did say hoochie dress. *Hoochie* happens to be my middle name.

Anyway, I was in the basement level, chillin' with some of the peeps around the indoor pool. The pool had a water-level brick bar going along one entire side of it. There was also a sitting area with a leather sectional sofa and bearskin rug in front of a huge fireplace with a roaring fire.

I was sitting on the sofa, tore the hell up, listening to the kicking-ass music coming from the speaker system wired into the walls. Some girl was trying to talk me into letting her eat me out, and to be honest, I was about ready to take a walk on the wild side. I hear a woman can eat pussy just as good, if not better, than a man. Sutton walked up behind us and eavesdropped on our conversation.

He stated his objection. "Ladies, no need for all that. It would be my pleasure to devour both of you!"

"That's what I'm talking about!" I was quick to reply because he was definitely my type of I-don't-give-a-flying-fuck-what-you-think man. "I get to go first, though. Bet?"

The other girl got mad. Apparently, she was strictly about the nana and didn't want a man doing shit for her. She got up and walked away, cussing under her breath. Didn't faze me one bit, since that meant more tongue action for me.

After thoroughly checking Sutton out from the top of his slick, bald head to his bulge to his satiny smooth skin, I was ready to get busy. He was about six feet even, built, and F-O-I-N-E. The bald head just did my ass in, though, 'cause that's my weakness. He was wearing a pair of swimming trunks and nothing else, which suited me just fine.

I was ready for him to dig right in and start eating me like the fabulous and delicious feast I am. Instead, he took me off guard. "Let's take a swim!" With that, he left me on the sofa, walked away, and jumped into the pool. The way he squeezed his nose and yelled out before he jumped in reminded me of little boys jumping off a wooden pier at a lake.

I decided what the hell. Following a good dick around is a small price to pay for hellified sex. So I seductively got up from the couch and pulled my dress up over my head as I switched toward the pool. My little show was not only for Sutton's benefit but also for the other men in the room to witness. For a hoochie like me, every move I make is carefully planned out to be sexy, and my entire life is a masquerade.

I continued my little show by sitting on the edge of the pool with my revealing thong bikini on and splashing the water around with my perfectly manicured toes. I used my hand to fling my hair back over my shoulder, and all eyes were on me 'cause I got it like that.

Sutton was over by the pool bar. I got all the way in the pool and swam across it with the grace of a swan. He was ordering a drink from whoever was standing in as bartender at that moment. The guy behind the bar appeared to be drunker than everyone else put together. Sutton ordered a rum and Coke and asked me what I wanted. I told the truth: "I want you!"

Our eyes met, and he started blushing. I turned toward the bar and asked for a frozen strawberry daiquiri. I made sure to ask for an orange slice and cherry, so I could show off my oral skills, and boy, did I. While Sutton was watching, I took the cherry, arched my neck back, and slowly dipped it into my mouth, sticking my long, pink tongue out to meet it. Then I chewed it seductively, just the way I perfected it when I practiced at home on a regular basis. I followed the cherry up with the big finale, the orange slice. I took the orange slice and put it in my mouth, letting the rind fill out the entire outline of my lips, and then sucked on it and whispered, "Yummy!"

It was time for my pitch. "I wonder if anything on you

tastes as yummy." My eyes were locked on his dick like a missile locked on an enemy fighter jet.

He was still blushing. "Well, there's only one way to find out!"

I kept my head down, but flashed my eyes up at his. "Ummm, do tell!"

Sutton took me by the hand. We carried our drinks along the ledge on the wall of the pool until we got to one of the corners. I pressed my back into the contour of the corner, sat my drink on the tiled floor surrounding the pool, and propped my elbows on the edge of the pool so my breasts would look even more enticing than they already are.

He put his hands around my waist after setting his drink down also. "Now, what's all this shit you've been talking, missy? I bet you're all talk and no action, just like all the rest."

I took one of my hands, placed it in the water, and started rubbing his dick through his swimming trunks. "Try me!"

The pool had at least twenty people in it and another dozen or so standing around, who all ended up getting an added treat when Sutton and I turned the house party into a live sex show.

As our kisses began, Sutton picked me up, and I locked my lengthy legs around his waist. He wasted no time untying the skimpy top of my bikini, removing it, and letting it float away on top of the chlorinated water. I leaned my shoulders back as his head moved down to discover the sweetness of

my dark, hard pearls. While he was sucking my nipples, I noticed the same girl who had offered to eat me out standing
on the other side of the pool, glaring at us. Thank goodness
looks can't kill, or I would be one dead hoochie.

After a few moments of him feeding off my breasts,
pouring some of the frozen daiquiri on my nipples and
sucking it off, I unwrapped my legs and stood down in the
pool. I gave Sutton a peck on the lips and then disappeared
underneath the water, pulling his swimming trunks down
as I went. He kicked his trunks completely off, and they
too ended up floating on the water. I took his dick in my
mouth underwater and started sucking on it. When I took
it the entire way in and started deep-throating it, the echo
of the water intensified his moans.

I stayed down there as long as I could without taking in
too much water with my nose and then popped my head
back up above the surface. I wasn't surprised to see everyone was paying avid attention. More people had joined the
crowd from upstairs and the pool outside. I could understand the thrill; I love to watch other people getting their
freak on myself.

Sutton told me to turn around, so I did, and put my
hands on the edge of the pool while he ripped my thong
off and threw it on the tile. He started caressing my rotund
ass cheeks and pressing his dick up in between them. Then
he pulled my ass out toward him some more, knelt down
a little in the water so the head of his dick could find my
pussy lips, and pushed it up in me.

I reached my right hand up over my shoulder and

started rubbing his bald head while he fucked me slowly underneath the water. He picked up a steady pace, reached around, and started pinching my nipples. I loved that shit!

People were saying things like, "Damnnnnnnnn!" "Look at this shit!" and "You go, girl!" Then there were the sexually repressed and threatened women who were urging their men to leave or go to another room so they couldn't watch. As usual, I didn't give a fuck about any of them, 'cause I was getting mine.

The sensation of being fucked underwater made me cum within minutes, but Sutton kept working his dick in me until my moans grew so loud, I almost scared myself. About ten or fifteen minutes later, he finally came all over my water-covered ass.

We spent the next few minutes caressing each other all over and asking some of the pertinent questions we should've been asking before we fucked, like name, marital status, involvement situation, etc. After getting all that out the way, we realized neither of us had any balls and chains, so it was all good.

Sutton suggested we get out of the pool and go sit by the fire. As we walked over to the seating area, men were giving him high fives and slaps on the back like crazy. Most of the women were staring at me, but my friend Faye, the one giving the party, was laughing her ass off. "Page, you're just too wild, sis!"

I just looked at her, curled my lips into a smile, and kept on going. Sutton and I sat down on the bearskin rug by the fire, water droplets still covering us both, since we hadn't bothered to dry off with towels. I started rubbing his dick up and down the shaft, hoping it would get hard again.

After some well-spent effort, it did, and he fucked me again on the rug in front of everybody. He took my ass the second time around. People are a trip. They always talk about the things they would never ever do in a million years, but are gung-ho when it comes to watching it.

Sutton and I dated for a few months, but he was in the military and was sent overseas, so that was the end of it. We had the time of our lives while it lasted, and I miss him terribly. However, life goes on, and so did my sexual escapades. You can't keep a sexual diva like myself down.

I only have one piece of advice. If you have a good man with a good heart and, most important, a good dick, don't let other women anywhere near him. One of these days, you might fuck around and let a nymph like me in the front door. Scary thought, huh? I'm only one of many, so you better watch your back!

Wrong Number

"I'm sorry, you have the wrong number!" It started with a wrong number and ended with the fuck of a lifetime. It was about seven o'clock on a Wednesday night, hump day, and I was worn the hell out after a hard day at the office. My live-in boyfriend, Tony, wasn't home yet. It was his night to play basketball with the boys at the gym. I was sitting there on the couch with my legs up, sipping on a glass of red wine and watching *Judge Judy* while I was waiting for my chicken breasts and baked potatoes to finish baking.

At the time, Tony and I had been living together for a little over a year, and it was all good. Things were going well between us. The lovemaking was very satisfying. I don't know why I did what I did, and I'm not trying to make excuses for it. All I can say is, I had fallen into kind of a rut. Let's face it, shit happens!

When the phone rang, I figured it must have been my

mother or one of my girlfriends but had no idea, since the caller ID was in the bedroom. I picked it up and said, "Hello." The man on the other end of the line said, "Hello, may I please speak to Stacey?" I told him, "I'm sorry, you have the wrong number!"

He then asked, "Is this 555-2269?" and I said, "No, this is 555-2268." So he said, "Sorry, my mistake. Have a good evening!" and I replied, "You, too. Peace!"

Now, you would have thought that would be the end of it, but naw. About a half hour later, *Judge Judy* had gone off, and *Real Life Stories of the Highway Patrol* was on, where they show people getting their asses arrested and shit in real life. They have cameras all up in their faces. It's mad funny to me for a person to not only get caught in the act but cold busted on TV in front of millions of people as well. Anyway, I had just taken the chicken out of the oven and thrown a pouch of boil-in-the-bag rice into a pot on the stove when the phone rang.

I assumed the same thing I did the first time, must be my mother or one of the girls. Wrong again, because he called my ass back. I don't know what the fuck happened, but I ended up flirting with him on the phone for over an hour. He had a deep, mesmerizing, sexy-ass voice, and frankly, the shit turned me on.

Why I told him my name was Amber, I have no idea. Probably because it was the logical response to him telling me his name was Rob. He just made me feel so comfortable and at ease. There I was, kicking it with some stranger on the phone about everything from the latest Puff Daddy and the Family CD to our respective careers to my hair appointment the next day. He and I talked about the fact that there are so few black barbershops and hair salons in our predominately white New England town. I happened to mention that I used a stylist named LaLa at this salon called She Thang over on Twelfth Street.

Even though the conversation was stimulating, I finally told him I had to go because it was getting late. He asked me could he call again sometime, and I said, "Absolutely hell fucking no! My boyfriend would kill me if nuccas started calling the house for me while he's home!" He said he completely understood and that it was nice meeting me, even if it was only over the phone, and insisted on asking one question before we hung up. I asked what the question was, and he asked me to describe what I looked like.

I told him that I was five-nine, 145 pounds, and light-skinned, with shoulder-length medium brown hair, and half Native American. He told me, "You sound delicious!" He volunteered his information before I could even ask and told me that he was six-one, 190 pounds, and dark-skinned with hazel eyes. I told him what was on my mind and replied, "You sound delicious too!" That was it except for the formal good-byes.

I made love to Tony that night and fell asleep in his arms fantasizing about a nucca named Rob who I knew by voice and description alone. I was so aroused that I couldn't sleep. I woke Tony up in the middle of the night by sucking on his dick, and it was all good.

The next day at work was a typical Thursday. I'm a

human resource manager for a construction company. I left about an hour early, after changing into some casual clothes, so I could get to my 5 P.M. hair appointment on time. I beat the work traffic and got there ten minutes early. Of course, when I got there, LaLa had one client in her chair, one under the hot-ass hair dryer waiting for all that dayum gel to dry up in her finger waves, and another one sitting in the lounge area with a magazine, waiting to get shampooed. I was not fucking surprised, since hair stylists always overbook and shit to ensure they keep clocking dollars whether everyone shows up or not.

I finally got my touch-up in about an hour later. I was sitting in the chair at LaLa's station, waiting for her to blow-dry me, when the phone rang at the salon. One of the other stylists, this big-ass girl named Shakia, told me that the phone was for me. I was dumbfounded, wondering who in the hell would be calling me at the hairdresser.

I went to the telephone, and it was Rob. I was fucking shocked. He told me that since I said he could never call me at home again because of Tony, he knew calling me at the salon was the only chance he would ever have to speak with me again. He said that he was only about twenty minutes from there, and he couldn't resist knowing I was going to be coming out looking good with my hair just done and wanted to drive over and meet me.

I was so scared, thinking to myself, "Is this man crazy?" I was hoping his ass wasn't crazy, but figured what the hell. I might as well take the chance, since I was in public. If I didn't feel right, I would just leave his ass there.

About thirty minutes later, LaLa was done with my hair, and he had not shown up, so I was contemplating leaving. I was sitting there flipping through some magazines when he came bouncing in the door, plopped down right beside me, and smiled this big ole grin. I couldn't help but do the same, because the man was too dayum fine.

I was a nervous wreck because everyone was looking. I walked outside quickly, and we stood in front of the salon talking for a few. He asked me if I would like to go to a restaurant down the street called the Cuckoo's Nest and I accepted. I was tripping hard because this was totally out of character for me. My ass walked down there with him anyway.

We were seated at a table in the corner. I asked him to excuse me while I went to the ladies' lounge to freshen up, but that was not the real reason I needed to leave the table for a few moments. I had to call Tony and make up an excuse for being out so late. I called him from the pay phone in the hallway leading to the restrooms and explained how I had run into a girlfriend at the hair salon, decided to go out for a couple of drinks, and would be home about midnight.

I came back to the table and became lost in Rob's voice, eyes, and the whole package. Time seemed to fly by. It was 10 P.M. by the time we finished our meal and went through two bottles of nice Chablis. We left the restaurant and walked back to the pay parking lot where both our vehicles were located. I started up my Honda Accord and decided to sit in Rob's Grand Cherokee while I was waiting for it to warm up. I assumed the night was ending there. I had to work in the morning and knew I was already in trouble, but somehow talking turned into kissing. We sat and kissed and hugged and kissed and talked and hugged some more.

I told him I really had to get going. He leaned over for a final kiss and then whispered in my ear, "I don't want you to leave tonight!" He laid this kiss on me that made me melt, so I turned off my car, got back in the truck, and asked, "Okay, so now what?"

The parking lot attendant had been watching us from his booth a short distance away the whole time. The kissing and hugging went on for a good hour, and I couldn't take it anymore. I told him I knew about this really secluded lake about five minutes away. Off we went with a quickness.

After we got there, he started kissing me again and feeling all over my breasts. That drives me wild because my nipples are the most sensitive part of my body. I was so wet, I could feel the juices squishing between my legs. I had on this thin jogging suit, which wasn't helping matters any.

I figured we weren't going all the way. I'd just give him some hellified head, and that would be that. I unzipped his pants and put my lips to work. He leaned back in his seat and moaned and begged me not to stop. He was getting ready to cum when he said, "Hold up!" Then, all of a sudden, he put his hand down my pants from the backside and pushed his fingers in me, and that was it. I was done! He had me from that point on, and the shit felt *soooooo* good.

Rob said, "I can't let you do me and not return the favor!" He got out of the truck, came around to my side, opened my door, and swung my legs around. He pushed my shirt up and pulled my sneakers and pants off and threw them on the floor of the truck. He spread my legs open and started eating my pussy like a man on death row devouring his last meal.

I kept saying, "Ohhhh, Rob!" I was at a loss for any other words. It was dead quiet out that night. There were no cars. Just the sounds of nature and me and him moaning and ooooing and ahhhing. Then he went into a bag he had in the back of his truck, pulled out a condom, and put it on. He reclined my seat and starting fucking me like there was no tomorrow. I came SOOOOOO HARD! I wanted to scream, but I was still holding back because I really didn't know this man from Adam.

He stopped before he came, had me get out the truck, and bent me over. I was leaned over on the seat with my feet on the ground when he did it to me from behind. I loved that shit. My ass must have been shining in the moonlight, but I didn't even care at that point. He came, and I came again, and needless to say, my new hairdo was sweated the hell out.

We put our clothes back on. I was feeling like a whore, since I had never done anything like that before. He drove me back to my car, kissed me good night, gave me his number, and that was it. Even though the events of the evening were totally uncharacteristic of me, I look back on it now with no regrets because everyone needs to release their wild side every now and then. Men do it all the time, you know what I mean?

Tony and I are still together. I called Rob once, a few

days after we fucked in the moonlight by the lake, and asked him did he think I was a slut. He said, "No! In fact, it just makes me want to see more of you!"

Sitting here now, recalling all of this and becoming horny as hell for him all over again, only one thought comes to mind. Dayum, maybe I need to call him tonight and see what he's doing!

Room 69

I arrived in Charlotte on a Monday night about 9 P.M., rented a car at the airport, and got checked into the hotel by ten. I was exhausted. It was a cold and rainy night in December. I forgot to pack an overcoat or umbrella before I left California, so I was soaked and freezing by the time I got in the room. The room they gave me was cozy and had a nice king-size bed. I laughed when the clerk handed me the room key because it had the number 69 on it. That brought all kinds of interesting thoughts into my head.

I had been to Charlotte before on business trips and always had a boring time in the evenings. I didn't know anyone there outside of business, and so most nights, I would just grab a pizza or sub and eat in the room, do a little work on my IBM ThinkPad, and go to bed.

There had been one exception. About six months before this particular trip, I had ventured out and gone to breakfast with a man I met at a business meeting. We had a nice breakfast, and then he showed me around town in his car, kissed me good-bye on the cheek, and that was it.

After I got back home, we talked on the phone quite often. Both of us joked about how the chemistry was there between us, and yet we were both too nervous to act upon it. I told him if I ever ran up on him again, I would fuck his fine ass on sight. He agreed it was definitely a plan of action because he was feenin for me, too.

I was so cold and damp when I got in the room. I decided I would just take a warm shower and call him in the morning to discuss the possibilities. Needless to say, that's exactly what I did. I called him the next morning at work, and he was elated to hear from me. We made plans to meet up at my hotel after I had completed my business meetings. We planned to go out to dinner around six in the evening.

When I got to the hotel, he was parked in front of my room and leaning on his car, awaiting my arrival. I was about ten minutes late. I decided to stop by a drugstore and pick up some condoms. There was no way I was gonna let anything disrupt the plans I had to get busy.

We went into my room and chatted maybe ten minutes, if that, and then it was on. I enjoyed being with him because he was very passionate. He kissed me with conviction, and his tongue made me melt. We lay there in each other's arms for a good while, just enjoying exploring each other's mouths.

Then, he got up from the bed and turned off the evening news, saying he didn't want any noise distracting our lovemaking. The room was completely silent except for the faint noise of the heat escaping from the vents, an occasional car door slamming, and the distant clatter of someone getting ice from the machine in the courtyard.

He came back to the bed and pulled my black cable-knit sweater up and over my head, removing it. He kissed me again, this time even more sensually than before. I remember thinking he was the greatest kisser I had ever known. I imagined his tongue tracing patterns on my pussy lips, on my clit, and inside my pussy walls. Having oral sex performed on me is always the highlight of any fuck session for me. I anxiously awaited the point in time when he would quench his thirst with my nectar. I just knew the moment was coming, because that was all he ever talked about during our phone conversations. How much he wanted to taste me. I could tell by the way that he explored my mouth that he would probably be a prime candidate for the Pussy Eaters Hall of Fame.

He lowered my bra straps and sucked on my nipples, getting to know each one of them up close and personal. I pulled his head up so I could kiss him again because it was such a helluva turn-on. I pushed him on his back and straddled myself on top of him, letting my breasts dangle over his mouth. He grabbed both of my breasts, pushed them together a little roughly, and licked all over them at the same time.

I took his tie and shirt off and licked all over his chest, using the tip of my tongue to carve a path from his nipples, down his rippled chest, to his belly button, where I paused to dab my tongue in and out of it. I bit gently on his nipples and rubbed them around between my thumbs and fore-fingers.

I unfastened his belt buckle and pulled his pants down and off, untying and removing his shoes during the process. I helped him remove his red silk boxers and started sucking on the head of his dick before they even hit the floor. His dick was so good. I enjoyed feasting on it until he climaxed. His hot cum trickled down my throat, lining my stomach with a warm coating.

The moment had finally arrived. I just knew it was my turn to lay back and relax while he got to know me orally. Boy, was I wrong!

He fell asleep, calling the fucking hogs after only a blow job, and I was pissed. All the anticipation and planning for nothing. I caressed his dick, hoping to arouse him from his slumber, but nothing.

It was only about 7 P.M. at that point. I realized a hard day's work can be draining, but dayum him. He slept until almost eleven, four fucking hours, and when he woke up, I was sitting at the table over by the window going over some figures on my laptop and drinking some wild-cherry-flavored springwater.

I gawked at him with disbelief when he told me to come back and join him in bed. Then I figured, oh well, maybe he was just tired. Now he was gonna do all the shit he claimed he wanted to do to me on the phone. I went back over and lay down on the bed. I had my bra on, having repositioned the straps so my breasts were covered, and my black pants and panties were still on. He hadn't even touched me down there.

Once again, he started in with the kissing, but this time, I wasn't as receptive. The impression was already embedded in my mind that he wasn't even worth my time or effort. He did the nipple thing again, and I was bored.

Finally, he got to the bottom half of my body and started rubbing my vagina through the material of my pants. He pulled them down and off. I was thinking, "About dayum time." He was finally gonna get busy and eat my coochie-coo.

Wrong! He started finger-fucking me. I wanted to tell him so badly that finger-fucking went out with bell-bottoms, Afros, and platform shoes, but I tolerated it, hoping it was all a means to an end.

Once again, I was wrong, so I decided to get the whole fucked-up situation over with. I got a condom out the box, slapped that shit on him, and rode him real fast until his ass came. He had the audacity to try to stop me, grabbing my hips and saying, "I don't want to cum yet!" I wanted to say, "Fuck you!" But that would have been dumb, considering I was fucking him—lousy fucking, yet fucking all the same.

I finally got his ass out of there about midnight, after explaining to him why he couldn't spend the night. I had an early meeting in the morning. I was too through and couldn't believe I built his ass up in my mind to be some black Don Juan when he wasn't 'bout shit.

You probably think I just took my ass to sleep depressed or went back to crunching numbers on my computer, huh?

Nope! My ass was starving, since he and I never made it to dinner, and I hadn't eaten anything except a bagel with cream cheese about 8 A.M.

I took a shower, got dressed, and went to check out this all-night diner. I had noticed it two exits away in the vicinity of the drugstore where I bought the condoms. What a joke! I should have left them bad boys in the store and had a V-8 instead.

The diner was practically deserted when I arrived at a quarter to one. It was a Tuesday, so most people were home snuggled in for a good night's sleep, making love to their mates, or watching late-night repeats of talk shows like *Jenny Jones* and *Jerry Springer*. If it had been a Friday or Saturday night around the same time, I'm sure the place would have been packed with people who'd developed the munchies after a night at the movies or dancing and drinking at a club.

There were only a few other people scattered around at the tables—some black guy over in the corner suffering from an obvious case of jungle fever, a couple of teenage boys laughing loudly and trying to see which one of them could be more obnoxious than the other, and a black guy in a booth by the window who appealed to me right away.

Why he appealed to me, I'm not sure. He was attractive, but I see attractive men all day, every day. Maybe I was just still feeling horny, sexually repressed even. I still couldn't believe that man talked mad shit about how he was gonna turn my ass out and managed to do nothing but turn my ass off.

The guy in the booth was very nicely built and looked very friendly. I sat there sizing his ass up while I waited for some ditzy waitress named Becky to bring my grilled chicken breast sandwich with fries. He was mocha with dark eyes, a sexy mouth, and juicy-ass lips. I imagined drawing the bottom one into my mouth and sucking on it. Next thing you know, I was wondering whether or not he had a big dick.

I snapped out of it when tactless Becky slammed my plate down hard and asked if I wanted a refill on my iced tea. I was tripping, sitting there fantasizing about freaking some man who had only stopped by a diner to get a bite to eat. He wasn't thinking about my ass. Or was he?

As I was sitting there hitting the hell out of this bottle of slow-ass Hunt's ketchup to no avail, I felt his eyes on me and looked up. Sure enough, he was staring dead at me. He smiled at me, I smiled back, and the wheels started turning in my head. I began to ponder exactly how scandalous it would make me if I picked this guy up and whether it would classify me as a certified hoochie if I did. I let out a sigh of relief when he got up from his table, placed a tip on it, and headed toward the front door.

The ball was no longer in my corner, since he was taking his ass home and going to bed. The night turned out to be full of surprises, because he paused at the door, which his hand was holding halfway open, allowing a cool breeze to come in, and then turned around and headed straight toward my table.

My heart started pounding a mile a minute. The shit was

un-fucking-believable. He came up to me and said, "Excuse me. You have a minute?"

I looked up at him and managed to utter one word, "Sure!" He sat down across from me and just stared me in the eyes, and I was a nervous wreck. He just sat there grinning at me for what seemed like an eternity. In actuality, it couldn't have been more than a couple minutes.

Finally, he asked, "Aren't you gonna eat?" I told him my appetite was gone, and I thought I was hungry when I placed my order, but it was much too late at night for me to actually eat. It was all bullshit, but there was no freaking way I was gonna have him sitting there watching me chew my food.

We started chatting about whatever. I told him about my career and he explained how he was stationed nearby in the military and had just gotten back to the states from a long assignment in Panama.

Then, he just happened to mention the fact he hadn't had any pussy in a good while and wondered if he could have some of mine. I freaked. My first instinct was to cuss his ass out, but I didn't. Instead I asked him what he meant by "have some." He wanted to know what the hell I was talking about. I decided if his ass could be blunt like that, my ass could do the same thing.

So, I laid it out for him and told him how I expected this turn-my-ass-out, toe-curling sexual experience, and what had really happened instead. I told him how much I love having my pussy eaten and how I felt like the shit I did a few hours before wasn't even fucking. Then I asked him whether or not he just goes downtown to window-shop or does he actually purchase something.

He started laughing because of the way I phrased it. I asked him, did the laugh mean he wasn't about shit either? He leaned closer to me over the table, took my hand, and adamantly stated that he loved to eat pussy and would love to eat mine. Again, I froze; I couldn't believe the shit was happening. I left California to go on a *business* trip, and all I was worried about was having my coochie eaten.

After a few moments of silence, he inquired whether I was fronting or not. The man was dead serious about going down on me. He told me he would follow me back to my hotel room in his car and lick me clean. I couldn't help but blush. Normally, I would have hauled ass and run for the hills, but there was something about him. He had such a friendly disposition and seemed like a good old country boy who would eat me like a pot of chitterlings with Tabasco sauce.

I pondered and pondered while he waited and waited for a response, telling me to make sure I was comfortable with it before I made a final decision. Becky kept coming over, asking if we wanted anything else, and we both repeatedly said no. I think she was just being nosy. As empty as the place was, she knew we didn't come in together and figured there was some freaky-deaky shit going on.

Finally, I decided I was a grown woman, and hell yeah, I did want my pussy eaten, was feenin for it even, so I told him to bring it on. He paid my check at the counter, left Becky a tip, and walked me to my car, asking one more time if I was sure. I told him I was very sure.

He followed me back to the room and chuckled when he saw the number on the door. It was three in the morning. Once inside, he told me straight up he wanted to see me naked. I took my clothes off, since there was no point in turning back.

After I was butt-naked, I got up on the bed and embarked upon the wildest oral experience I've ever had. The man was all about the pussy. He was a beast. First, he sniffed all around it like a predator in the woods seeking out some prey. He told me how much he loved my aroma and was glad I was clean. I asked him were there some women who really had bad personal hygiene habits. He replied with a loud "Hell, yeah!" telling me sometimes he could smell a woman's pussy when he walked by her on the street because the odor was so strong and funky. I could do nothing but laugh and tell him I was glad I passed the inspection.

Then came the interesting part. Instead of just spreading my legs open and cleaning my clock, he positioned himself beside me on the bed, lifting my right leg up in the air and putting my thigh up on his back with his head facing toward my left thigh instead of directly at my clit. He lifted my left leg up in the air and pushed it outward so that my legs were spread wide apart and started eating me.

Boy, did he eat! All I can say is the man was starving like Marvin. I lost count of how many times I came. He was not lying—he loved eating some pussy, unlike the sexually disappointing fuck who had been on the very same bed not long before. After a while, my left leg, which was hanging out there in the air, started getting tired. I put it down on the bed. He immediately pushed it back up and told me to hold it there.

I wasn't used to holding my leg up like that. Normally, the man's shoulders would be holding them both up. Instead, his back was holding up my right one, and it was mad comfortable, but my left leg was having problems. He unzipped his jeans and guided my hand to his dick. I started jacking him off, even though that wasn't in the contract. It was cool with me. I was kind of lying there with nothing to do with my hands, so what the hell.

He ate and ate, and I jacked and jacked, and he ate some more until the moment of truth arrived and he detonated. Scared me shitless, too. He came so hard and made these sounds like a fucking animal. Never in life have I seen anything like that before or since.

He passed out right there, with his head in between my legs. The right one was still resting comfortably on his back. The left one was cramped up, but holding its own, since it could finally lie flat on the bed.

The shit was too wild, and I wasn't about to go to sleep, not knowing a dayum thing about the man, so I flipped through cable channels all night with the remote while he drooled on my pussy and enjoyed his slumber.

At 7 A.M., I told him I needed to get ready for a meeting. He woke up, turned over onto his back, and started rubbing all over his own chest and up and down the shaft of his dick. I thought to myself, "Oh, shit! Now his freaky ass is gonna masturbate in front of me!"

He did play with himself until he came. I watched it. It was sort of interesting. Besides, a woman doesn't get to see such a command performance often. Then he got up and asked me did I want his number. I replied with, "Sure, why not?"

He wrote it inside a matchbook cover with the hotel name imprinted on it, and I saw him to the door. I couldn't believe I had done that shit, but bottom line, the first guy wasn't 'bout it, I got what I craved in the end, and it was all good.

I took yet another shower, threw on a navy business suit, went to my meetings, grabbed a pizza on my way back to the hotel, ignored the messages the clerk gave me from the lousy-ass fuck who was all talk and no action, and went to bed.

I flew back to California the next day, none the worse for wear, and now I'm sitting here writing my scandalous, yet sexually fulfilling, escapade down in my journal. It may be a long-ass time before I have something this interesting to write in here again. Then again, maybe not! The fact of the matter is, as wild as it was, I truly relished it, so I have learned my lesson. Before that night, I would've told everyone I wouldn't do something freaky like that. The lesson that I've learned is to never say never again.

The Dick You Down Crew

They were known as the Dick You Down Crew. Women across the nation spoke of them in whispers and sometimes even in code. Women who had actually experienced them sometimes resorted to speaking about them in tongues. There were three of them: the Wishmaster, the Lickmaster, and the Dickmaster. The Wishmaster was the one who granted your every wish and helped you to live out your every fantasy. The Lickmaster was just that: a master at licking you wherever and whenever it pleased you. The Dickmaster was, aw Lawd, what can I say? He was the master of pleasure, pure and simple.

I saved up for eleven months to acquire their services. Once I hit twenty-nine, it became painfully clear that the man of my dreams was not going to come along. The thought of turning thirty without ever really having an earth-shattering orgasm was too much to bear. So I saved and I saved until I had accumulated the necessary five thousand to hire them for the evening. I know five grand is extravagant, but after all I had heard, I felt it was well worth the investment.

I made the initial contact through their website, www.dickyoudowncrew.com, and received an instant reply from an autoresponder. It informed me that my inquiry had been received and that someone would contact me within forty-eight hours. I actually fabricated half the information on the form I was required to fill out. I don't trust the internet, no matter how secure they claim it to be. I am one of those sisters who print out the mail-order form instead of ordering online at those e-commerce sites. Sure, I can get things faster if I do the real-time credit-card processing, but I prefer to wait the extra time and play it safe.

I lied about my name. I said it was Chiquita Locksley instead of Laura Connelly—same initials but reversed. I used my free email address instead of my regular one with my real name attached to the end of every message. I had to put down a phone number, so I put in my cell phone. If things got out of hand, changing it was nothing but a thing because less than a dozen people had the number in the first place. Besides, my live-in boyfriend would have had a fit if someone called me from dickyoudowncrew.com and left a message on the voice mail.

I know. I know. I said that the man of my dreams had not come along, and he hadn't. That didn't mean I was determined to go without sex altogether. Puleeze, that was not even an option. I was living with Scott, and most of my girlfriends were crazy jealous—but if they only knew. Sure, Scott was fine, brilliant, successful, and drove a seriously fly car. The convertible Jaguar had always been in my top three for the bomb-ass-car-of-all-time award. That's how he managed to pull me. I was walking down the street during rush hour, and he almost ran my ass over in the crosswalk. My first instinct was to cuss his ass out, but when he got out of the car and I got a look at him, the sun started shining even though it was forty degrees and dismal a moment before.

He was fine. True, that. Six-one, tight body, deep chocolate skin, and a smile that could light up a room. Little did I know that he was seriously lacking in the sex department. The first time we threw down, I wasn't even sure that his dick was in until he started yelling, "I'm cuming!" I wondered how the hell he could be cuming when I hadn't even begun to get my freak on.

It must seem strange that I ended up living with him, huh? Well, to be quite honest, Scott was good at some things, like sucking on my breasts—which happened to be one of the greatest turn-ons to me—and sucking on my toes. Besides, I adored his mother and the rest of his family. His sister and I had become the best of friends over the three years we had been together. Yet and still, I needed something extra in my life. I needed to be fucked six ways from Sunday.

I only made thirty grand a year at my administrative job, but I managed to come up with the five thousand I needed. I asked Scott to cover all the bills for a few months, and he happily obliged. I think it made him feel more like a man, having a woman dependent on him. I realize my methods were shady, but hey, I needed the money before I lost my damn mind for real.

For the next two days, I patiently waited for a phone call. One time my battery went dead on my shitty-ass cell phone. Why do they lie and say that a battery has a long life when they know it sure as hell doesn't? As soon as I had it up and running again, I checked for voice mail messages, and there was a message from this dude named Joe. I didn't feel like being bothered with his ass.

Joe had been my first "creeping" experience during my lackluster relationship with Scott. He talked big game but turned out to be just that: all mouth and no action. I got naked, and he acted like a scared bitch. For a second, I thought the fool might have been a thirty-three-year-old virgin, but he got his act together and did a little sumptin' sumptin'. Still wasn't worth my time, effort, or ribbed condom, though.

I was juggling three paper grocery bags and my brief-case up the stairs to our second-floor apartment when my cell phone rang, exactly forty-eight hours after I had hit the submit button on dickyoudowncrew.com. In my haste to catch the call, I dropped one bag and heard the carton of eggs splatter on the outdoor carpet.

"Hello," I breathed heavily into the phone in disgust.

"Is this Chiquita Locksley?"

What the hell was this? There was a woman on the other

end of the line. Surely, she couldn't be the Wishmaster or Lickmaster, and she damn sure couldn't be the Dickmaster unless she was working with a strap-on.

"Who is this?" I demanded to know.

"This is Robin."

"Robin. Hmm, I don't think I know a Robin."

Looking back, I don't know why I was frontin'. The odds of some sister ringing my damn cell phone, having the wrong number, and happening to ask for my recently created alter ego were slim to none.

"Once again, is this Chiquita Locksley?" she asked in a pleasant enough voice. "Did you fill out an information request form on dickyoudowncrew.com?"

"Umm, yes I did." I put the bags down and put my key in the lock, making sure to avoid stepping in the egg yolks that were all over the place. I hesitated for a moment and peeked over the balcony to make sure Scott's Jaguar wasn't in his assigned space. I didn't want to go inside if he was home, because he was the nosiest brother on the planet. "I filled out the form, and I've been waiting for you to call."

"Sorry for the delay, but we get a ton of requests, and sometimes the staff gets a bit overwhelmed."

I managed to get myself and the groceries in the house, opting to clean up the mess in front of the door later.

"Hmm, you have that many women asking to get put on, huh?" I asked, wondering if it was such a good idea after all. I mean, damn! How many sisters had these dudes knocked off?

The sister on the other end of the line started laughing. "Well, the men are rather popular. It seems that the word has really gotten out lately."

"So, how much is it?" I already knew the price but decided to ask anyway, in case they were running some specials. In fact, I asked, "Are you running any specials?"

She laughed again. "No, sorry. We just have the flat rate of five thousand a night."

"What exactly constitutes a night, and what services are performed for the five thousand?"

I could've sworn I heard a lip smack on the other end of the line. No, she wasn't tripping on me all of a sudden. We were talking about five thousand damn dollars.

"Didn't you read the description of services on the website?"

"Yes, I did but it didn't define 'night' to my satisfaction. Are we talking a certain amount of hours, sunset to sunrise, or what?"

"You get eight hours. Additional hours are available upon request, but there is a fee."

"And how much are the extra hours?"

"Five hundred an hour."

"Damn!" I exclaimed into the handset.

"Is there a problem, Chiquita?"

"No, no problem." I collapsed onto the sofa, wondering if I was doing the right thing. After all, five grand could stretch a long way at my favorite mall. Fuck it, I was going for it. "So, when can I get an appointment?"

"Hmm, let me check."

There was a brief silence, and I could hear paper shuffling on her end.

"We have Tuesday, July ninth, available."

"That's a month from now."

"Yes, I know, but it is our only available date. Would you like to be scheduled or not?"

"Yes, yes, I'll take it," I answered excitedly. This was going to be more interesting than I imagined. July 9 was my thirtieth birthday.

"Cool. I need to get some further information from you, like where you would like the gentlemen to meet you. I'll assume you want them to come to your place?"

"No, no, no! They can't come here!" I yelled in a panic. Imagine that. Scott coming home with roses and a birthday cake, only to find me ass out with three men slapping skins.

Robin didn't skip a beat. "What city and state are you in?"

"Chicago, Illinois."

"Not a problem. We have various hotels that we work with throughout the country. We have several there in the Chicago area. I will email you a list, and you can make the appropriate arrangements."

"Hold up. Are you saying that I have to pay for the room?"

"If you want a room, you have to pay for it. The five thousand simply covers the sexual favors and travel expenses."

"Fine," I stated nastily. At least they weren't trying to take me for plane tickets, meals, and all that shit.

"Wonderful. You will have an email within the hour

detailing our rules and regulations, a list of local hotels in your area, and payment instructions. All monies must be received at least seven days before your appointment."

"Okay, whatever."

"Thank you for your time, Chiquita."

Just like that, Robin was gone.

July 9 was the strangest day of my life. Scott woke me up with his tongue. Now Scott had licked a lot of things in three years, but he had never licked my pussy. But there he was with his head buried between my legs, going to town on my coochie. I didn't have a lot of experiences to compare that one to, but he seemed to be doing okay with it. He wasn't making my thighs tremble or anything like that, but it was interesting.

"Happy birthday, baby," he whispered about ten minutes after I'd opened my eyes to his surprise. "Thirty years old. You're about to be over the hill."

"The hill you crossed over four years ago, huh?" I asked jokingly.

"Hey, that was a cheap shot."

Scott tickled me until I was screaming for mercy.

"See, that'll teach you not to make fun of a brother's age," he said after finally letting me go.

"You started it," I childishly replied.

He reached over and retrieved a small black velvet bag from the drawer of the nightstand on his side of the bed.

"Seriously, happy thirtieth, Laura." He handed me the bag. "This is something special for someone special."

I took the bag and just stared at it. What on earth was he up to?

"Laura, open it already." Scott laughed.

I undid the drawstring on the bag and pulled out a black velvet box. At that moment, I knew the thing I had most wanted and dreaded at the same time was about to happen. I tried to think quickly, but instead my mind went completely blank.

Scott took the box from my hand and snapped it open, revealing a two-carat diamond ring. It was stunning.

"So, will you?"

I was speechless. My eyes fluttered from the ring to his face and back again.

"Laura, will you do me the honor of becoming my wife?"

I didn't know what to say, so I said the first thing that made sense. "Can I have some time to think about it?"

The look of disappointment on Scott's face was nothing short of depressing. We sat in silence for a couple of minutes before he asked, "How much time do you need?"

"Just a day or two," I replied hesitantly. "It's just that I wasn't expecting this."

"But what do you have to think about, Laura? We've been together for three years." He set the ring down on the comforter and gently took my hand. "Don't I make you happy?"

"Yes, Scott, you make me happy," I said halfheartedly. "I still just need a little bit of time. Cool?"

"Cool."

Scott got up from the bed, and while he didn't exhibit anger in his movements, I knew he was fired up inside. He had taken the ultimate step to commitment, and I had shot him down.

He got dressed, and as he was leaving, he asked, "Do you want to go out to dinner tonight to celebrate your birthday?"

"Umm, I can't." My lies were about to begin. "I promised my mother that I'd spend tonight with her. Like you said, this is a big day, and she really wanted to do something special for me."

"Kind of like I tried to do this morning," he said.

I ignored his comment. "In fact, we might be out kind of late, so I'll probably just spend the night and head to work from there in the morning."

"Laura, all I can say is, enjoy your birthday, and I guess I'll see you when I see you."

Scott walked out the bedroom, and a few seconds later I heard the front door slam.

Taking the day off from work was a given. My boss was not a happy camper about it, but that was his personal problem because I never, ever work for the man on the day of my creation. I spent the morning being pampered at a day spa. If I could put out five grand to get laid properly, I could splurge on a pedicure, manicure, hairstyle, and massage. By one o'clock, I was walking out of the spa on pillow-soft toes and looking fly as shit.

I lucked out and found a spot in front of my favorite

lingerie store. I selected a hot pink satin bra and thong set, even though I didn't anticipate having it on too long.

While I was standing in line to pay, I called my mother from my cell phone to do an intervention. If she happened to call Scott for any reason to discuss making plans for my birthday, my ass was toast. I told her that I would be spending a quiet, romantic evening with Scott. She was disappointed but felt better once I promised her that we would do lunch the following day.

By three, I was ready to check in at the luxurious downtown hotel that I had selected from the list Robin emailed to me. It was actually the most expensive, but anything worth doing was worth doing right. The men were not due until eight, and that was cool because the nervousness had set in. What the hell was I doing?

The room had one big-ass bed. I read the card placed on the pillow and couldn't believe the prices of the bedding offered to guests that wished to purchase items in the gift shop. Eight hundred dollars for a down comforter? Only big ballers could roll like that. For one night, I was going to be a big baller. A big baller surrounded by big dicks.

Once I got settled into the room, I realized that I was about to starve, so I trotted down to the hotel restaurant. I was all about splurging that day, but the prices for their food were ridiculous. Thirty-two dollars for a steak, and then you had to pay for the potato and vegetables separately at five bucks a pop. I didn't even think so. I took my ass right down the street to Hooters and threw down on some wings.

Men are hilarious. Every time I go into a Hooters by myself, they look at me like I'm crazy. Shit, good food is good food. Besides, women walking around in tight-ass tops and barely clothed bottoms is no different than a day at the beach. Scott and I had gone there once for lunch, and he was so embarrassed that he was ready to leave before the food arrived. I explained to him that a man looking at tits and ass flashed in his face was perfectly normal, and I would've been more concerned if he wasn't looking at them.

I returned to the room with a full stomach and ran a warm bath with some vanilla sugar bath gel, my favorite. I had been tempted to get a cup of chili with my meal, but the last thing I needed was to be all gassed up when the Dick You Down Crew arrived. Normally I only shower in hotel rooms, but since this particular one was so pricey, I was hoping their cleaning was thorough and on point.

I drew the shades, dimmed the lights, and sank into the tub. I had Jill Scott doing her thing on the CD player/radio beside the bed, and I took a little time to get myself ready for the action later that night. Masturbation has always been a major aspect of my sex life. Without it, I would've gone cuckoo years before. Besides, there's nothing like pussy that has been simmering in juice for a while before a man hits it. It's like comparing a marinated steak to one thrown on the grill straight out of the package.

I cupped my left breast and rubbed my nipple with my thumb while I fingered myself with my right hand. I lost myself in thought as I tried to decide what wish I would request of the Wishmaster that night. There were so many fantasies that I had never lived out. That in itself was a damn shame. Somehow, I would have to narrow it down to just one, and it was a toughie. So I ran the different scenarios through my mind as I masturbated, and finally there was one that made me climax like a clap of thunder. Yes, that was the one I would ask for.

I sprayed myself down with body oil after my bath and put on the lingerie, or "lingeree," as they call it in the hood. Before I knew it, I had dozed off. A knock at the door stirred me back awake about an hour later.

"Oh, my gosh!" I exclaimed as I catapulted up off the bed. The reality finally hit, and I asked myself, "What the hell am I doing?"

Scott had proposed to me that morning, and I shot him down. He might not have been perfect, but he loved me. He'd even shown it by going downtown that morning for the first time. I knew that was a big hang-up of his, but he had done it anyway.

Then there was my mother. Why was she popping up in my head when I was about to fuck three men? Because I had lied to her for the first time in years, and I should've been spending my thirtieth birthday with her and my man. Instead, there I was in a ritzy hotel with three men on the other side of that door who had come to smoke my boots.

I inched my way to the door, took a deep breath, and flung it open, expecting to see the Dick You Down Crew. Instead I saw an old-ass man whose eyes were about to pop out his head. I immediately ran to the closet to get a white hotel robe to throw on.

"Who the hell are you?" I asked after covering up.

He grinned at me, and I could almost see the nasty thoughts running through his head. "Maintenance. Did you call about a blown-out lightbulb?"

"No, no, I didn't call."

He started trying to smooth down his dirty coveralls and smooth back his even dirtier hair. "Maybe I should just come in and check you out. I mean, check it out."

I glared at him with disdain and tried to shut the door. "I didn't call about a bulb, so leave me alone before I call downstairs and report you."

The expression on his face went from lust to fury as he pressed his hand against the door. "All that ain't even necessary. I thought this was the right room. Can't fault me that you answered the door half-naked."

I tried to knock his hand off the door. "Just leave."

"I will as soon as you tell me you ain't calling downstairs. I need this here job. I got eight kids at home."

I was dying to ask him what kind of woman would birth eight of his children, but refrained. I just wanted him to go away. He looked to his left toward the bank of elevators and sucked his teeth. "Damn, what have we got here? Is the Mr. Olympia Competition in town?"

I peeked around the corner and saw them: the three finest brothas I'd ever seen in my entire life, and they were headed my way.

I looked back at Mr. Nasty. "Look, I'm not going to report you, all right. Just leave and enjoy the rest of your day."

The three men stopped right in front of my door, hovering over him because he was blocking their path.

The tallest of the three asked, "Chiquita?"

"Yes," I quickly responded.

Mr. Nasty lifted his clipboard and perused it. "Chiquita? It says here that your name is—" I slapped my hand over his mouth, which he swatted away. "What on earth is wrong with you, girl?" He looked up at the three men and back at me. "Maybe I'm the one that should be reporting something to the front desk. An assumed name. Three men showing up at your door. Are you a hooker?"

"Hell, no, I'm not a hooker!" I yelled in anger. "Now leave before this gets ugly."

One of the other men asked, "Is everything straight here?"

Mr. Nasty moved out of their way. "Everything is everything."

I also moved to the side so they could all enter the room. "Look, I'm not sure which room needs a lightbulb, but it's not this one. Thanks for your effort, though."

I tried to be nice so he would drop the hooker theory, although he wasn't far off base. I just didn't happen to be the hooker. I was the john.

Mr. Nasty moved closer to me, and his foul breath almost did me in. "Listen, after you're done with them, what can I get for fifty dollars?"

I smacked him in the face. "Get the fuck away from my door!"

He rubbed his face and took off down the hall, turning around just long enough to spew the word "bitch."

After closing the door, it hit me that *they* were in the room. The Wishmaster, the Lickmaster, and the Dickmaster. I was alone with the Dick You Down Crew.

I froze and could barely breathe. One of them walked up behind me and started massaging my shoulders. It felt incredible. He leaned over and whispered in my ear, "Relax. Whatever drama just happened, whatever fears you have, whatever brings you pain, all of them are about to disappear, because the Wishmaster is here."

"Damn, the Wishmaster," I whispered before glancing up over my shoulder at him. He was the tallest one, and a tall drink of water he was. Deep chocolate with a bald head and a smile that could make women melt.

He swept me up in his arms and carried me over to the bed to lay me down. The other two, who were equally fine, were standing by the window. They didn't have any luggage, just briefcases. They probably discreetly had rooms booked someplace else where they would relax after knocking me off.

After laying me on the bed, he started rubbing my feet. Thank goodness I had taken the time to get a pedicure—if my toes had been jacked up, I would have been ashamed.

"So, tell me, Chiquita . . . tell *us* what you would like to happen here tonight."

"Um . . . I don't really know," I said. "What do you usually do?"

"Whatever is asked of us." He glanced at his two friends.

"Each of us has his own specialties. Of course, I make wishes come true, so what's your wish?"

"I actually gave that a lot of thought before you got here."

"And?"

"I want to know what it feels like to have someone in all three holes at one time."

He grinned, and I could hear the other two chuckling. "That's easy enough. The only question is, can you handle it?"

I was honest. "I don't know but I'd like to try. I've never personally tried it, but I saw it once in a porno film."

"And it turned you on?" he asked.

"Yeah, it did, but my boyfriend would never agree to something like that. In fact, he would probably kill me if I even suggested it."

The Wishmaster lifted one of my feet to his lips and ran his tongue over the underside of my toes. "Well, he's not here tonight, so he doesn't matter."

I started trembling for some reason, probably because of fear. This was really it, and while the thought of having all three holes hit at once was arousing, it was also down-right scary.

The shortest of the three, a light-skinned brother with hazel eyes and wavy black hair, came over to the bed and stood over me. He reached down and palmed a breast in each hand. "You need to relax. The Lickmaster is going to loosen you up a bit. How about that?"

I didn't respond. I just allowed him to lower my bra

straps, exposing my nipples. He rubbed them between his fingers for a few seconds and then reached below my back to unsnap my bra. He took it completely off and then leaned over me to suckle on my nipples. I could see his dick, his *huge* dick, through the tan slacks he was wearing. It was leveled right above my head.

I knew that an opportunity such as this would never come my way again, so it was time to let go of all my inhibitions. While he continued to work his way back and forth from breast to breast, squeezing tightly the one he didn't have in his mouth, I reached up and undid his belt buckle. I toyed with his zipper until I got it down and pulled his dick out. He teased me with it by lowering it just enough for me to taste it with the tip of my tongue and then lifting it back up out of range.

I have to admit that it made me laugh, because he was making me indulge in some strategic moves to get to the dick. Finally, I just grabbed it and started milking him like a leech. Apparently I must have been on the money, because he moaned and then ripped my panties off so he could bury his head in my pussy.

He climbed up on the bed with me, placing his knees beside my shoulders. That's when I did something I'd never imagined doing. I actually licked the brotha's ass. It was kind of tart, but you could tell that he was clean. Some of my friends have spoken about eating their men's asses, but the thought had always appalled me. Not that night.

The Lickmaster matched me tit for tat by moving his head even farther down so he could eat my ass out, too.

He had the thickest tongue in the world and knew how to work it. He definitely deserved his title.

Through my peripheral vision, I could see the other two getting completely undressed. I almost gagged on the dick that I had put back in my mouth when I saw the size of the one on the Dickmaster. This wasn't a myth. His dick was really down to his knees. He was fine as shit, just like the other two. Caramel with a fade and dark bedroom eyes. His dick looked like two feet of smoked sausage. I couldn't wait to dig in, but I was a bit leery about him sticking it up in me. I envisioned it going in my pussy and coming out my mouth.

I didn't have to wonder long because he came over and tapped the Lickmaster on the ass. "Let me get in there, dog."

The Lickmaster sat up and wiped his lips. "Girl, you've got it going on. Some sistahs don't eat right, and let's just say, their pussies are kind of rank, but yours is on the money."

I took that as a compliment, even though his descriptions were kind of raunchy. For five thousand, I thought he would be more cautious about his choice of words.

The Dickmaster went around to the opposite side of the bed, spread my legs wider, licked all of his fingers in one swoop, and then rubbed them over my pussy. He stuck one finger inside and said, "Um, nice and tight."

The Wishmaster chuckled. "Not after you get done with it, homey."

Those words hit home, and I propped myself up on my elbows. "Listen, I'm not trying to get ruined for life. You can't stick all that in me."

The Dickmaster hooked his arms under my knees and pulled me closer to the edge of the bed. "Relax. You're going to love it, and you'll never forget me."

I started thinking way back to my sexual health class in high school. They always said that a woman's vagina could conform to handle large items and then pop right back into shape. After all, babies come from there, and most are about two feet long at birth.

That helped me out a little, but my thighs still started trembling when the tip of his dick hit my clit. I closed my eyes and braced myself for *the dick*. He eased it in a little at a time until he had it about halfway in. That was my limit!

"No more," I pleaded. "I can't take any more."

He held himself inside me for a minute, rubbing my ass cheeks and licking his lips. Then he started going for it, and all I can say is, it hurt, but it was a good kind of hurt. He pulled out before he came and exploded all over my tummy.

After that, we all took a shower together, which was a feat in itself. Three big-ass men and little ole me in a shower doing all sorts of freaky things. I sucked off the Wishmaster, who ate me out in return. Then the Lickmaster lifted me up against the tile wall and banged the hell out of me there. I was going to attempt to give the Dickmaster a blow job, but decided I was simply not up to the task.

After we got out of the shower, the Wishmaster kept his promise and made my wish come true. I could never describe the intensity of it, so I won't even try. It was the ultimate sexual experience to have a dick in my mouth, in my pussy, and in my ass at the same time. Miraculously, I was even able to walk the next day.

I called in to my job and told them I needed another day off. Much to my amazement, my boss didn't have an attitude for a change. He even wished me a happy birthday, and it meant something even though his was a belated one.

I went home and crawled into bed. Scott was at work, thank goodness. I had no idea what to say to him, so it was just as well that he was gone. I slept all day and woke up with Scott standing over me, staring at me.

"So, Laura, have you thought about it?" he asked without so much as a hello first.

"Yes, I thought about it," I lied. I hadn't been thinking about anything but other men's dicks since I had seen him last.

"And what's your decision?"

I didn't respond.

"Laura, I have been here for you for three years. If I haven't proven that I love you, that I live for you, that I would die for you, then maybe I don't need to be here."

"Scott, I—"

"Fine, just forget it. Just remember that no man is ever going to love you as much as I do. Not ever."

He was right about that. No one would ever love me as much as him, which is why I blurted out, "Yes, I'll marry you."

A huge grin spread across Scott's face. "Really?"

"Yes. Want to pick a date?"

Okay, so maybe Scott isn't perfect, but he's all mine. I love him, and he loves me. We're getting married in the spring, and I am actually looking forward to it. While the relationship might be lacking in certain departments, no one is perfect. This is as perfect as it gets, and if I ever feel like I need more, all I have to do is log onto www.dickyou downcrew.com.

The Bachelorette Party

I knew my gurls were gonna throw me a party the night before I jumped the broom, but dayum. They went all out for my bachelorette party. After the rehearsal dinner, I figured they were going to take me to one of my bridesmaids' houses and have a stripper or something. I couldn't have been farther off base if I tried.

Instead of taking me to a house, we drove about an hour out of town to what appeared to be an abandoned warehouse. However, there were tons of cars outside and people walking in and out the front doors, mostly women.

When we went inside, it was the wildest shit I had ever seen. Dick for days! Days, I tell you! I had been to my share of strip shows in my day, but I had never been to one where all the men were dancing butt-naked. There was no sign on the door, but once inside, there were neon signs everywhere with the club's name, the Black Screw, on them.

The gurls and I, about ten of us all together, found a

couple of tables in the rear, since all the tables up front had long been taken. A waiter came to take our drink orders, and the man was fine as all hell. I wanted to lick a piña colada off his ass, but I refrained from my nasty thoughts. After all, I was marrying the love of my life the next day, and faithfulness was a must. It was hard to keep the faith with the waiter's big, juicy dick dangling in my face, though.

A few minutes later he returned with our first round of drinks while this other fine-ass guy with about a ten-inch dick was sitting in my maid of honor's lap, blowing in her ear. I was totally shook and couldn't believe I never knew the place existed. It had to be some undercover club because mad laws must have been thrown out the fucking window in order to have all that dick floating around the room.

The Black Screw was huge, too. Imagine a warehouse turned into a big-ass fuck palace, and then you are half-way there. "Doin' It Again" by LL Cool J kicked in, and this fine-ass guy (hell, they were all fine) took center stage and began to do some of the most amazing acrobatic fuck moves I had ever witnessed. The way he was pretending to grind his dick in some nana made me wanna scream, Have mercy! He continued with the grind moves until the song ended, but when "Big Daddy" by Heavy D came on next, he got buck-wild and buck-naked. Dayum shame all those big dicks were in the house.

The gurls and I got tore up by the third round of drinks, and by the fifth round, we were all horny. I was sitting there wishing I could get my hands on my fiancé's ass right then and there, because I would have fucked him like I hated him. I'm not quite sure who was wilder, the male dancers or the women patrons. There was some truly freaky shit going on up in that place.

Men had women bent over tables, grinding their dicks up against their asses, they were palming tits, sucking toes, fingering pussy even. As for the women, aw shit, they were even worse. The women were pulling their shit off too, jacking dicks, riding dicks with their clothes on, everything except actual fucking, but don't take my word on that. I didn't exactly do a panty check or anything of that nature.

One man after another took the stage and did his thing. I must say there is no way any woman who even remotely loves herself some dick wouldn't be drowning in her own pussy juice up in the Black Screw. There was a stage right smack in the middle of the club, like a boxing ring in the middle of an arena, with tables surrounding all four sides of it so all the women could get a little look-see. In addition, there were circular risers in the four corners of the club with male dancers, who had already performed and taken it all off, on them getting mad freaky. I'm telling you, the shit was all that! They were so naked the only place they could put the dollars women tipped them was in their boots. I noticed they were all wearing some sort of boots, mostly cowboy ones. Cash-and-carry, I suppose.

As much as I loved it, it was getting pretty late. Two A.M. was rolling around, and the wedding was at noon sharp. I told the gurls we should bounce and thanks for taking me there. My maid of honor, Shari, told me the party wasn't over and then called the fine waiter over and whispered something in his ear. I sat there nervous as all hell because I figured they were planning on having some guy come over to the table and freak me or something. I had managed to keep my hands to myself all night, even though the temptation was killing me.

About five minutes later, the waiter returned with three other waiters and a cake. While our waiter set the cake—which, by the way, was chocolate and shaped like a huge dick—on the table, the other three clapped and recited some rehearsed congrats-on-your-wedding verse. I was relieved that the cake was the surprise and loosened up a bit.

My relief turned to panic when the finest guy in the place walked up to me. If Mother Nature made anything better, she kept him for her dayum self, because the man was hitting. He was about six-four, 210 or 215 pounds, dark-skinned, with jet-black curly hair and deep brown eyes. He stood out in the club because he was clothed with stonewashed wide-legged jeans, a suede vest, and of course, cowboy boots.

He leaned over the table, reached for my hand, and I was likely to faint. Shari told me, "You better get your ass up!" I asked her, "What the fuck is going on?" She replied, "Just a little something extra I have planned for you! This is your last night of freedom. Now, GET THE FUCK UP!"

You could tell from the expression on her face that she could barely prevent herself from breaking out into a full grin. I was drunk, and his hand was still reaching out for me. I threw caution to the wind and took it.

A couple of minutes later, he and I walked through a set of double doors into the rear of the Black Screw. He had yet to say a word to me. I figured Shari had paid him to give me a private dance, sort of like a male lap dance. To be honest, I was still nervous as shit, though. If he had been just average, cute, or even remotely fine, I would have had no problem whatsoever. The problem was, he was past all those, and I was tore up. My pussy was throbbing and shit for him just by the hand-holding alone. I was getting the distinct feeling my ass might get in some serious trouble once he did his little show. I should have stopped it right then. I should have told him I felt uncomfortable and was about to rejoin my friends so we could leave. But I didn't, and before I knew it, we reached our final destination.

There was a long hallway in the back of the club with several rooms. All the rooms had neon signs over the door-ways. He led me to one called "The Red-Light District" and held the door open for me to go in.

The room was dimly lit with red lightbulbs, and there was a slow jam playing. Much to my surprise, there were four couches in the room, one on each wall, and two of them were occupied. I tried to pull my hand loose after I saw what was going on in the room, but he held onto it tightly and spoke to me for the first time: "Don't run away, baby. At least let me do my dance for you. Don't worry about them!"

He had the deepest, sexiest voice, and when he looked

at me with them there eyes, I was at his beck and call. So, I didn't worry about *them* and went and sat on the couch farthest from the door while he walked over to the compact shelf stereo system and changed the CD. *Them* referred to the two other female customers in the room with male dancers. There was absolutely no dancing going on, and when my private dancer was putting on his performance music, I could hear *them* moaning and shit. Not to mention the fucking and sucking noises.

You see, one sister was over on the couch by the door, and her ankles were pressed up over her shoulders while a big, Mandingo-looking brother was fucking the shit out of her. The other was not quite as bad. However, she was sitting on the couch on the left wall sucking another brother's dick like a Hoover vacuum cleaner. Apparently, the lap dances they received were slamming, because they were all about knocking boots.

All sorts of shit started going through my mind faster than the speed of light. I know I should have been thinking about my baby, my boo, my husband-to-be, but he never crossed my mind. In fact, looking back on it now, I don't feel guilty because I know about all the shit that goes on at bachelor parties. His ass probably fucked some hoochie that night too.

He put on his music, "My Body" by LSG, and began his dance. He told me, "My name's Warren, by the way. What's yours?" I told him, "My name's Mira," as he began to do his thing, grinding all in my face while I sat there on the couch with a serious case of locked knees.

Warren slowly removed his vest, and like I had suspected, he was perfect. I tried to keep my eyes fixed on him, but it was hard with all the other shit going on. The other two couples had done some shifting, and the one who had been sucking dick was now bent over getting fucked doggy-style. The other one, who previously was shaped like a pretzel, was now in the sixty-nine position getting her freak on.

I began to feel light-headed as Warren started to break out of his jeans. I recuperated fast when I saw his dick protruding out his black thong bikini. Just like I like them: big, long, thick, and chocolate. That was the very moment I knew I was gonna fuck him if he was down. Judging by the way he was looking at me, I suspected he was.

Warren confirmed my suspicions when, once naked, he knelt down and pried my knees open with his strong hands, exposing the black lace panties I was wearing underneath my black knee-length skirt. I wore no stockings with my heels because it was midsummer and extremely hot out, so it was easy for Warren to run his fingers all over my smooth, creamy thighs. He began to kiss my kneecaps. All I could do was look, being I was overcome by a desire I had never known, a desire to make love to a complete stranger. A desire, it appeared, I was destined to fulfill the night before I married the man of my dreams.

That is exactly what I did. I fulfilled the desire to make love to a stranger, and I have not regretted it a moment since. In fact, I think the night with Warren has significantly helped my married life. I know that sounds sick, but I was able to open up more sexually with him than I could previously do with my boo. Because of the events of that one night, I have become a much better lover for my man.

Warren started running his tongue up and down the inside of my thighs, spreading my legs wider with his hands. My pussy was soaked by that time. He pushed me back on the couch, so I was lying down, pulled my panties off, and then lifted one of my legs up so it was resting on the headrest of the couch.

He wasted no time getting his eat on with my pussy as the main course. I thought I had died and gone to heaven because I came like crazy. The wild part is that I didn't even give a fuck what the other people in the room were doing. That's totally uncharacteristic of me, because I tend to be very inhibited. At least, I was before that night.

His warm, thick tongue played magnificent tricks within my pussy walls, and I got lost in the music and the red lights while he did the thing he does so well. He reached up, with his head still buried between my thighs, and caressed my tender breasts through the white poplin-sleeve blouse I was wearing with the black skirt. I took the initiative, unbuttoned it for him, and unfastened the clasp in the front of my bra, letting my hard nipples escape their prison.

Warren moved his tongue from my pussy, over the material of my skirt, which was up around my waist at the time, and started sucking on my nipples. I went fucking berserk. I'm not sure whether it was the liquor or the fine-ass nucca licking me all over, but I just kept cuming and cuming.

I'm not sure when the other couples got up and left the

room. I didn't see them because I was too busy sucking Warren's dick, which was, by the way, extremely pleasing to my taste buds. I sucked him so good he exploded in my mouth twice before we moved on to the main event—the main event being knocking boots.

The man fucked me every which way but upside down. If time had permitted, we probably would have gotten to that position eventually. I needed about three days to fuck him the right way. Instead, I only had about three hours. We made good use of them, though, and he tore my coochie-coo up. He gave a whole new meaning to the phrase "dick-whipped."

Never before, or since, have I ever begged a man to stop fucking me because it was too much for me, but I begged his ass to stop grinding his dick into me in such a fashion. Warren didn't let up, though, and ended up giving me the fuck of a lifetime.

When I rejoined my friends, after quite some time, they were about the only ones left in the entire club. Some of the gurls had left already. The only ones remaining were the ones I was riding with, including Shari, my maid of honor. They were all laughing and grinning at me. I didn't even attempt to fake the funk because there was no way they would have believed I had been back there talking for the past three hours plus.

I did the next best thing and told them all about it on the way home in the car, blow by motherfucking blow, and they were all ears, probably envisioning every second of it the way I related the story to them.

By the time we got back to my hotel suite, the sun was coming up over the horizon. I only had an hour to get to my hair appointment, so I showered and dressed and headed for the land of hot-ass hair dryers and curling irons. At noon on the dot, I walked down the aisle of the church I had attended since I was baptized in it and married my boo.

I exchanged vows with him and meant every word of them. I love him dearly and would never forsake him for another man again. Like I said earlier, though, I think the night with Warren improved my bedroom skills, and therefore has helped keep my marriage together. My boo thought he was marrying his shy, conservative baby, but on our wedding night, he found out he married a sexual diva.

I can't say for sure what men do at bachelor parties, but I can say this. Any woman who has her bachelorette party at the Black Screw is in for one hell of a great time!

The Pussy Bandit

I was always told to eat everything on my plate.
Well, the bed is my plate.
Ladies, may I fellate?
—the Pussy Bandit

No one knows his name or what he really looks like. In the middle of the night, he sneaks into his select choice of the evening's dorm room, ready to strike. He feasts on his meal and then leaves as quietly as he came. He bequeaths a single long-stemmed rose on the pillow of yet another woman who'll never be the same. The small New England university for women I attend is his hunting ground. Every student is his potential prey. No one ever complains, though. In fact, most women want him to stay.

We sit in our dorm rooms at night, giggling and wondering who'll be next. We always make sure our coochies are clean in case it's our turn to pass his taste test. It's like jury duty. You never know when you'll be called. Many of us lie awake at night listening for footsteps in the hall. Some call him crazy, others call him fine. I used to just hope and pray he would hurry up and get to mine.

You see, there are not many eligible black men in our small New England town. Often we find a few good men and have to pass them all around. Lots of women at the school wait their turn, saying, "Dammit! Hurry up and suck on this, you Pussy Bandit!"

I first heard of the Pussy Bandit my freshman year. I thought he was imaginary, an old wives' tale, something for the freshman students to worry about, laugh about, joke about. It wasn't until I was returning home late one evening from a midnight movie that I gave any credence to his existence. My roommate freshman year, Kelly, and I saw a man in black clothing climbing out the second-floor window of an upperclassman dorm. His face was covered with the kind of mask ninjas wear. He jumped from the window and landed on his feet behind a bush. He raced off into night, and to say the least, we were horrified. We rushed to the front door of the small dormitory and banged on it as loud as we could, almost knocking a glass pane out with our fists.

A girl on the bottom floor came out of her room with a short nightie on and opened the door for us. We both started yelling at her simultaneously, telling her what we had just witnessed and running down the hall toward the stairwell. She chased after us as we bounded up the stairs, rushing to the aid of what we just knew was a victim of some sort on the second floor. All sorts of bad things were rushing through my mind. Rape, robbery, even murder.

When we reached the second floor, I couldn't help but notice the upperclassman who had opened the door was very calm while she followed behind us. She appeared to be giggling when she said, "Oh, calm down! It was just him!"

Kelly took the time out to ask her who she meant by *him* while I walked the hall, looking for the door that matched the window we saw him leap out of. I found it and started banging on it. A woman's voice came through the door saying, "Just a second!"

She opened her door with a smile on her face, saying, "I've just been had by the Pussy Bandit!"

Kelly looked as if she might faint, and I said, "What the fuck?"

The upperclassman who opened the front door for us hollered out, "You go, gurl!" She pushed her way inside the other girl's room, sat down on the dresser, and asked, "Was he all I have heard?"

Kelly and I went in too, sat down on the bed, and didn't utter a word. We wanted to hear what happened as much as the other girl.

The girl, who was named Mandy, started telling the tale of how the Bandit had crept into her window and eaten her out like all hell. She was so graphic and excited about all the details, I could have sworn she looked like she was under a spell.

After that night, I was no more good. Having my pussy eaten is like winning the grand prize on a game show.

Just about every other day, I would hear about a girl who was eaten in this dorm or that dorm. I knew my chances were slim, since all freshmen have roommates. I spent the remainder of my freshman year taking long walks in the courtyard late at night, hoping he would change his pattern and suck on me under the moonlight. *Nada!*

I went to summer school just so I could stay around campus, figuring my chances would be better, since most women had gone home. Boy, was I wrong!

He seemed to hit every coochie-coo on campus but mine. Kelly finally got eaten, afterward telling me she told him, "It's about dayum time!"

Sophomore year came and went faster than the speed of light. I had my own dorm room then, and a lot of sleepless nights. I swore to myself that I wouldn't say a thing if he would just suck on my bones like a chicken wing. Still, *nada!*

I went home that summer 'cause I had a work-study job. I worried about who was getting eaten while I was gone. Geesh, my clit was so hard.

Junior year rolled around, and on my face there was always a frown. I started trying to calculate how much pussy there could possibly be in such a small town. I knew I would be much more healthy, wealthy, and wise if I could just get his lips between my dayum thighs. Still, *nada!*

It was halfway through my senior year when he finally got to me. It's time for the real deal, so fuck all this poetry!

It was winter break, and most of the students had

already left for the holidays. I was one of the few left. I decided to stay and complete a term paper one of my English lit professors was sweating me for.

I worked on the paper until about 4 A.M. and finally had to lie down. I couldn't keep my eyes open another second without propping them open with toothpicks.

I had been asleep about thirty minutes when I was awakened by the smell of his cologne. When I opened my eyes, I realized there was a slight breeze coming in from the open window he used to come in. I never locked my window. I didn't want him to waste any time prying it open, if and when he ever got around to me.

I knew who he was right away. He was dressed very similar to the way he was the night Kelly and I saw him years before. He had on black jeans, boots, and a turtleneck. His face and head were covered with a ninja hood and mask. The only things visible were his eyes. They looked so serene and sensitive in the light of my desk lamp, the one and only light on in the room.

I spoke, even though I had sworn to myself I wouldn't. "Are you really the Pussy Bandit?"

He put his finger up to my lips, and I could smell the scent of aftershave lotion on his mocha-colored hand. All he said was "Shhhhhhhhhhhhh!"

He reached into his rear jean pocket and pulled out two black silk scarves and a black blindfold. I eagerly raised my hands above my head so he could tie my wrists to the headboard posts of my bed. All the years I had heard about him made me feel comfortable around him, like an old family friend who showed up unexpectantly for Christmas dinner. Ironically, it was almost something like that.

He covered my eyes with the blindfold, making sure I wouldn't be able to see his face once he removed his mask. He obviously couldn't eat my pussy through the mask, so the blindfold was no surprise. I had heard the details from enough women to know what the deal was.

I could feel his soft hands on my skin as he gently pulled my black lace panties off. The only other thing I had on was a big T-shirt with an athletic brand label on the front.

Before I knew it, he began to dine on his meal. I knew immediately he was all the things I had heard and more. He gave my pussy a tongue-lashing it will never forget. I have had my pussy eaten a lot, mostly by men who had no fucking idea what they were doing.

Years of practice had given the Pussy Bandit the gift of a silver tongue and the ability to lick a woman's belly button from the inside. His tongue was thick, juicy, long, and very, very hot.

He spread my legs open as far as they would go and then dove right in like a professional swimmer diving into an Olympic pool. He got straight tens across the board.

For those people who don't know the award-winning qualities of a good pussy eater, allow me to enlighten you. First of all, a good pussy eater never, and I do mean *never,* gnaws on the clit. It's true that clits do get hard, almost like miniature dicks. However, the clit is extremely sensitive and can't tolerate too much direct stimulation.

So, all you men out there bragging to your buddies

about how your woman tries to pull away from you while you're eating the nana because it feels so good need to wake the fuck up and recognize. Half of the time, women are trying to pull away 'cause the shit hurts.

Secondly, the mark of a good pussy eater is the ability to get up on the Big G. You know, the G-spot. If they can hit that with some smooth tongue action, all hell will most definitely break loose.

Last, but sure as shit not least, is the ability to interject toys and other things into the total pussy-eating experience. Like I said, the Pussy Bandit got tens all across the board.

He hit my G-spot with his tongue, and I thought milk was gonna spurt out my tits, even though I wasn't even producing any milk. Instead, so much cum came shooting out of my pussy that I was alarmed. I thought he had ruptured some hidden cum bank inside my coochie-coo or something.

I was squirming and trying to pull away, but not 'cause it hurt. The experience was nothing short of splendid. It was such a sensual experience, moans escaped my vocal cords and nothing at all came out. I just bit my bottom lip and decided to grin and bear it.

He got up from the bed and I heard him walking toward my private bathroom. I had no idea, nor did I care, what he was doing. I figured he had to take a leak, but he came back without doing that. Instead, I felt him lift my hips up and place a towel underneath my ass. I was mad wet and assumed he didn't want me to soak my bed with cum too much.

As it turned out, he placed the towel there and then poured something cold all over my pussy. I felt something sting me on my clit and then recognized the smell of mint-flavored mouthwash as it hit my nose. He set his sights back on my pussy and began suckling on it again, tracing his tongue through the baby-fine hair on its lips. The mixture of the stinging feeling of the mouthwash and his powerful tongue made me cum again, even harder than the first time.

He loosened the scarves around my wrists, and I was praying he was only doing it to change positions or something. I hoped he would let me sit on his face for a bit, but *nada!*

I yelled out, "Wait! Don't go!" I struggled to finish removing the scarves. I got them loose, jumped up off the bed, ripping the blindfold off in the process, and ran to the window. I got there just in time to see him hit the freshly mowed grass and run off into the night.

I had waited four years for him to pay me a visit, itching for the opportunity to brag about him just like all the others. I didn't, though. I decided to keep the overwhelming experience between the two of us. Years from now, I'll open up my college scrapbook to the page that holds a single wilted red rose—the rose the Pussy Bandit bequeathed on my pillow the night he showed me what a true pussy-eating was all about.

Masquerade

"Noelle, don't take it the wrong way, baby!"

"What other way is there to take it?" I reached over on the nightstand and retrieved a couple of facial tissues out of the dispenser. "You come over here and tell me you're dumping my ass, and I'm supposed to jump for joy?"

"No, nothing like that. I just hate to see you crying, so please stop." Pierce started caressing my right shoulder, as if that would help any. "Besides, I'm not dumping you. I just feel like we both need to see other people for a while so that we can explore other avenues."

"Explore other avenues?" My tears started to dry up, and the anger set in. "What the fuck do you mean? Other avenues?"

He jumped up from the bed and had the nerve to get a 'tude. "Look, Noelle, there's no reason for you to cuss at me. I mean, it's not like we're married, or no shit like that. You need to take a reality check."

"I just don't understand why you want to see other women."

"You want me to be honest with you, Noelle?"

"Honesty's always the best policy, so they say. Hell, yeah, I want to know the truth!"

"Okay, but I was trying to be nice about this." I couldn't freakin' believe that Pierce was doing this shit to me. After all I did to be with him, all the dinners I cooked for him, all the sacrifices I made, and his ass was kicking me to the curb. "I need a woman who is more—"

"More what?" My lips started trembling, and my nerves were wrecked. I was expecting him to say he wanted a woman with bigger titties or a bigger ass or a bigger bank account or some backass shit like that. Boy, was I wrong!

"I need a woman who's more freaky!"

"What the hell do you mean, more freaky?" That was the last fucking straw. I jumped up from the bed and got physical, taking the palm of my hand and shoving him in the chest. "You and I do a bunch of freaky shit!"

"We do? Like what?"

I felt a migraine coming on. "Well, I suppose if you have to ask, it must not be freaky enough."

"I guess not!" He headed out the bedroom and toward the front door of my apartment. "Look, Noelle, I'll give you a call in a couple of days. Cool?"

"You're really serious about this dating-other-people shit, aren't you?"

"Yes, I'm dead serious. I'm not saying I don't want to be with you, because I do. In fact, more than likely, I'll end up marrying you and having a house full of kids, but right now I need to get some things out of my system." *Damn him!* "I'll catch you later, boo."

He was out in the hallway waiting for the elevator when I peeked out my door. "Pierce, what about our date this Friday? The masquerade party at Trent's house?"

"I'm still going to go, and it's cool if you do, too. I think we should go separately, though." With that, Pierce stepped into the elevator and was gone.

I was devastated, depressed, delirious, pissed the fuck off even. I cried myself to sleep that night, but by the time the sun came up the next morning, I was ready to pay his ass back in spades. If he wanted freaky, I would give his ass freaky.

I arrived at Trent's house about midnight. People in wild-ass costumes and masks were everywhere. I decided to wear a black leather cat outfit with a tail and snaps in the crotch, and no underwear underneath. It was strapless and had a push-up bra built in, so my 40DD breasts were looking succulent. I had a leather whip attached to my hip. I made sure Pierce wouldn't be able to recognize me by wearing a feathered mask like the ones they wear at Mardi Gras, a black wig cut in a cool-ass bob, and white contact lenses that made me look like a straight-up freak. Freaky and sexy as all hell rolled into one.

Pierce was over in one of the dark corners, flirting with a couple of hoochies. I knew it was him, because he was dressed as a fireman. I had selected the costume a couple of weeks before, so he was easy to spot.

After downing a couple of Long Island iced teas and watching people dance and get intimate with each other in the designated dancing area, I decided to do what it was I came there to do and teach Pierce a lesson he would never forget.

I took a quick survey of the area and spotted the person I was looking for, Trent. He was dressed as the Phantom of the Opera, with a black tuxedo and cape on along with a white mask. Several of his friends were surrounding him and wishing him a happy birthday, since that was the whole purpose of the masquerade party from jump.

Pierce was one of the people crowded around Trent, and I kept my head down a little as I brushed by him. I cleared my throat and got ready to use the Jamaican accent I had practiced, walked up to Trent, and whispered in his ear. "Happy birthday to you, baby!"

He took me by the hand and looked me up and down, but didn't recognize me. He and I had only met a few times. He was a close friend of Pierce's from college. "Damn, do I know you, sexy lady?"

"Not yet, but you're about to get to know me." I reached down and started caressing his dick through his pants while Pierce and the rest of them hollered out typical macho things like, "Get that pussy, man," "Damn, man," and "She's hot for you, Trent."

"Really?" He started palming my ass and other people started looking on as well, including some of the women, who were instantly upset and jealous. "What did you have in mind?"

I pushed him down on a chair at one of the round tables covered with white linen tablecloths and then straddled myself over his legs, facing him. "Let me show you what I have in mind." I almost laughed because my Jamaican accent was the bomb.

I stuck my tongue deep inside his hungry and waiting mouth. He gladly returned the kisses, and I must admit, I knew right off the bat I was going to enjoy fucking the shit out of Trent's ass. I always thought he was fine anyway.

After we tongued the hell out of each other for about five more minutes, I got up and stood between his legs as I lowered the front of my leather suit, allowing my massive breasts to be viewed by everyone in the room. Miraculously, a silence befell the room, and the only sound that remained was the music. Ironically, it was "Do Me, Baby" by Prince. Everyone was in awe. I glanced around to look at Pierce, who was in a daze, before I decided to hold my left breast out for Trent to suckle on.

He eagerly took my hard nipple into his mouth and fed off it, slowly at first. Then he decided he wanted them both, grabbed a hold of each one, and rapidly moved his head and tongue back and forth from left to right. My pussy was getting so wet from all the excitement that I began to care less and less about who was watching. Besides, my identity was safe, and that was the beauty of it.

A waitress was walking past with a tray load of champagne flutes. I grabbed one and poured the champagne over my breasts so he could lick it all off.

The disc jockey cut off all the music so he could come

and join the crowd of people watching the show. Needless to say, there wasn't a single person on the dance floor. The only sounds left then were his sucking noises and my moans.

I unsnapped the crotch of my cat suit and climbed up on the table, lay in front of him, and spread my legs. I put the whip around his neck and pulled him closer to me. I told him he had to be punished for being such a bad boy and that he had two choices. "Eat my pussy, or face the whip!"

Trent started laughing and looked around at his buddies, who started ranting and raving again and giving each other high fives. "Shit, I'm not afraid of the whip, but I prefer the pussy!"

With that, he drew the clit of my freshly shaved pussy into his mouth and started sucking on it. My pussy juices were really flowing as he spread my lips apart so he could lick up and down the inside of each one, lapping up every droplet of my nectar.

Once Trent made me cum two or three times, I got up from the table and got down on my knees so I could get his dick out of his pants. The white contact lenses almost popped out my eyes when I saw how big it was. His dick was twice the size of Pierce's. I realized there was a whole new world I had been missing out on by tying myself down to one man.

I took the tip of my tongue and slid it down the slit on the top of his dick, savoring the precum oozing out of it and admiring the way the veins were popping out as it pulsated. I gave his dick the royal treatment and proceeded to give it a wax job with my mouth. I could only fit about four inches of it in my throat, other than the head, because it was so thick and juicy.

I heard some sexually repressed sistah yell out, "Oh no, girlfriend is not sucking his dick right in front of all these peeps?"

The hell if I wasn't! I sucked and sucked until my mouth was sore and he shot a hot load of cum down my throat, making a warm lining in my stomach. I sucked his dick soft and then kept at it until it was hard again.

Then I got up and climbed onto the table on my hands and knees, and it was all too obvious that I wanted him to hit it from the back. He grabbed a hold of my leather-covered ass cheeks and gently slid the head of his dick into my throbbing, wet pussy. I had to take a deep breath to brace myself for the rest of it, because I knew he was about to knock the bottom out of my pussy. That's exactly what he did!

Right there, in front of all his birthday guests, Trent fucked the hell out of me. I knew, at that moment, that he was the man for me and not Pierce. What started out as simple payback turned into pure, unadulterated lust, and I loved every minute of it. He fucked me so hard that tears started to run down my face from underneath my mask. Never has anyone fucked me so intensely, and I could barely stand it. It was a confusing mixture of pain and pleasure, and before it was all over and said and done, my ass was turned the fuck out, my mind was blown, and I was in love.

He tugged on the wig, trying to force my pussy back farther on his dick. For a moment, I thought my ass was busted. I got a hold of it just in time to prevent my light brown hair from being exposed. I took Trent's hands and put them on my breasts instead, so he could rub my nipples in between his thumbs and forefingers.

I sat all the way back on his dick and started riding it right there on top of the table, and both of us were panting and moaning. We fucked each other like beasts until we both exploded in unison and the tablecloth ended up covered with cum.

After he reluctantly took his dick out, I jumped up from the table and pushed my way through the crowd, my 40DD breasts still uncovered and bouncing up and down. Trent tried to run after me, but Pierce and the rest of his buddies were too busy bombarding him with comments, slaps on the back, and congrats for fucking the shit out of me in front of the whole crew.

I made it outside and took in some of the fresh, night air. I searched, through tear-drenched eyes, for the Toyota Camry I had rented so no one would see me driving my actual car. When I was pulling off, I saw Trent run outside and stop in the driveway, catching only a glimpse of my taillights.

I went home that night and fell asleep, dreaming about Trent. I woke up the next morning and took a long, hot shower. While I was in there, I fucked myself with the wooden handle of my back brush until I came all over the fiberglass surface of the bathtub.

* * *

For an entire week, I wouldn't answer phone calls from Pierce, who kept leaving messages asking why I never made it to the party because he was waiting for me. Lying ass! Finally, he got fed up and showed up at my door, banging and demanding to be let in.

"What are you doing here, Pierce?" After I opened the door just a little bit, he forced it the rest of the way open so he could barge in.

"What the hell do you think I'm doing here?" He was mad and obviously stressed. "Why haven't you been answering any of my calls, Noelle?"

"I've been busy, and besides, you were the one who wanted to cease and desist for a while so you could get your freak on with other women." I had endured more than enough of his bullshit.

He looked at me and pulled me down on the couch beside him. "Noelle, I made a mistake. I miss you, and I was a fool. I made the mistake of thinking the grass was greener on the other side, but you're the only one for me. I don't want to see anyone else. It's all about you and me, boo."

It was all I could do not to laugh in his fucking face. Instead, I just looked at him with a perplexed look on my face. "Let me get this straight. You think you can come in here and lay down rules and regulations, and once I accept them, you have the audacity to try to take it all back?"

"I love you, and I miss being with you. I thought I wanted some sex fiend, but all I really need is you. Your innocence is what's so truly special about you."

That's when I burst out in laughter. "Oh, really?" I paused before I continued, "Well, I hate to be the bearer of bad news, but I think there's something you should know."

Pierce got up and went in the kitchen to get a beer from the fridge, pretending that my last statement never came out my mouth. "Speaking of sex fiends, you should have seen what happened at the masquerade party. It was off the hook!"

I smirked. "What happened?"

"This girl showed up, someone none of us had ever seen before, and fucked Trent right there in front of every damn body. She was a straight-up freak!"

"Sounds like your kind of woman. You said you wanted freaky sex, right?" I didn't know how much longer I could maintain my composure, because it was mad funny.

"For the last time, I was wrong about that. Sure, she was sexy and out there, but I'm ready to settle down, have a couple of rug rats, and buy a white house with a picket fence."

He was serious, and I almost had second thoughts about what I was about to do. However, the shit he did to me was unforgivable, and I could no longer look at him in the same way. "Well, Pierce, I like things the way they are."

"Whaaa—what do you mean by that?" He was flustered.

"I think seeing other people is a good thing. In fact, I think it's a wonderful idea, and I've already taken your words to heart."

Pierce jumped up in my face with his typical male,

double-standard ass. "Are you saying you're already seeing someone else?"

"Not exactly, but I do have someone in mind." It was time to drive the knife in. "In fact, I fucked him about a week ago, and I loved the way he fucked me. He tore my little ass up and fucked me without mercy. He had a big-ass dick too."

I thought he was going to punch me for a second, but instead he just sat down on the coffee table and put his head in his hands. I went into the bathroom as I added, "In fact, you loved the way he fucked me too."

I heard him shout from the other room, "What the fuck are you talking about, Noelle?" I didn't answer him. Instead, I just came back in the living room wearing the black wig and white contact lenses. He leaped to his feet. "What the fuck? It was you?"

I giggled and crossed my arms in front of me while I leaned against the wall. "Yes, it was me. Truth be known, all this time you were saying I wasn't freaky enough for you, but it's the other way around. You're not anywhere near freaky enough for me!"

He balled his hand into a fist, looked at me with his lips trembling for a couple of minutes while the whole sordid madness of the situation sank in, and then left, slamming the door behind him.

I've never seen Pierce again. The friendship between him and Trent ended the day Pierce found out I was moving into Trent's mansion with him. I went back and claimed the man I really wanted. Trent was shocked at first to discover I was the woman who had turned his ass out, but he had been feenin for me the whole time, so it was all good.

Let this be a valuable lesson to all you men out there who don't know a good thing until it's gone. Never judge a book by its cover, and never underestimate the power of a woman, or else you might just find yourself by yourself.

Body Chemistry 101

His name was Professor Vaughn Mason. To me, he was simply heaven on earth. I was lucky enough to be in his organic chemistry class my freshman year at State. I started lusting after him the first day of class. One glance into his captivating bedroom eyes, one flash of his charismatic smile, and I was hooked.

I used to daydream during his class lectures, undress him with my eyeballs, and wonder if he was a tender or rough lover. During one of our lab periods, I almost spilled a beaker of hydrochloric acid on my thigh. I'd lost my concentration, fantasizing about milking his dick with my mouth.

After freshman year, I didn't get to see Vaughn that often. A wave here, a smile there, an occasional greeting when we passed each other on the steps or in the halls of the Natural Sciences building. It was depressing.

Senior year rolled around, and purely by the luck of the draw, I ended up snagging his student assistant position.

It was like winning the lottery. I would get to spend time with him, talk to him privately, and maybe even brush up against him on the sly every now and then.

So there I was, his assistant, and excited as I could possibly be about it. Vaughn, whom I never addressed by his first name to his face, was so dayum foine. He was about five-eleven, 180 pounds, deep chocolate with dark bedroom eyes, and had a sexy-ass bald head. His body, dayum, what can I say except the man was cut and looked like his muscles were chiseled out of stone. If ever there was a man who could make a woman's pussy get wet by looks alone, he was the one.

I had just celebrated my twenty-first birthday during the summer. He was much older than I was, about forty, but I never asked. When a nucca is that fine, who gives a dayum about a number? He had never married, but he was shacking up with some nurse from the university hospital. Did I care? Hell, naw!

You can never control the way you feel. Which is why what happened just two weeks into the fall semester was beyond my control. Whenever I reflect on that day, I realize it was the single most erotic experience of my entire life—one that I wouldn't trade for anything in this world.

I remember it so vividly, like it was yesterday. Vaughn had a faculty meeting that morning. I stayed behind in the chemistry lab to grade some exams for him. I was sitting at his desk, grading papers, and my mind began to wander as usual. I imagined him and me alone in the lab as we often were, but instead of just going about the course of a normal day, he had me bent over his desk and was fucking me doggy-style from behind. The thought of it made my pussy so wet.

Even though it was mid-September, it was terribly hot that day. The formfitting white button-down oxford shirt I had on with a navy above-the-knee skirt, white slouch socks, and a pair of Nikes, was clinging to my breasts. I had the windows ajar in the lab. The Natural Sciences building was one of the oldest on campus and without central air. The only real breeze in the room was coming from the box fan I had strategically placed on the top of one of the long laboratory tables.

The mere thought of his hands on me was driving me berserk. I masturbated in my dorm room all the time thinking about him, but on that particular day, I needed some fast relief and couldn't stand the thought of having to wait until I went home. I analyzed the whole situation like a silent movie in my mind. The faculty meetings would usually last at least two hours, and I didn't have a dayum thing to satisfy myself with. Unfortunately, I didn't tote my vibrator around in my book bag. I would have done anything to have it at that moment.

I locked the door to the lab and went to sit back down at the desk. I leaned back in the comfortable leather desk chair with the reclining back and swivel base. I closed my eyes and fantasized about him kissing me on my lips, and my hands suddenly became his hands. I caressed my nipples through the cotton of my shirt. They were ripe and hardened. I unbuttoned the top three buttons and pulled both of my nipples out so that they were protruding from my bra.

I licked my lips, fantasizing about Vaughn sucking on them one at a time. I threw one of my legs up on top of the desk and, pushing my underwear aside, began to finger my pussy. It was so hot and moist, longing to feel his tongue. I stuck one finger in at a time until I was working three of them inside. I still had my eyes closed. In my mind, Vaughn was feasting off my sweet, tender pussy.

Finger-fucking myself was pleasing, but it wasn't enough. I wanted to feel something deep inside my pussy walls. I took my fingers out and licked my pussy juice off them, savoring my own flava. I opened my eyes and took a quick survey of the lab looking for something, *anything*, to use to fuck myself with.

Most of the items, like the microscopes and Bunsen burners, were out of the fucking question, but suddenly I spotted something that would do the trick. As I got up from the desk, I peeped the wall clock and realized that Vaughn hadn't even been gone a good hour. I assumed there was enough time to finish myself off. I walked over to the closest lab table to the front and retrieved a large test tube, one that held 500 ml, and went back to the desk, positioning my leg back on the desk.

I moved my panties out of the way again and gently inserted the test tube into my pussy. I had it inverted so that the bottom, round part was the entry point of the tube. It was made out of unbreakable Pyrex, so I wasn't afraid it would break and cut me if I got too carried away. To be honest, though, even if the glass had been breakable, I was so horny that it wouldn't have mattered much.

The cool glass felt great as I slid it in and out my pussy. It even tickled a little. After I got a good rhythm going, I closed my eyes and began to fantasize about Vaughn again, imagining him sliding his hardened dick in and out my sugar walls. I began to moan as I caressed my nipples with my other hand, lifting one of my breasts as high as I could and flickering the tip of my tongue over the nipple. I moved the test tube in and out faster and faster and the pleasure was so intense that——

I never heard his key in the lock or the door open, but I heard it close. I opened my eyes, and he was standing there, with a look of shock on his face and his mouth hanging wide open. I was so embarrassed to be caught like that, with my leg on his desk, breasts hanging out everywhere, test tube in my pussy with juices all over it. I should have taken it out, gotten up, and fixed my clothes but something happened.

The look on his face was not one of disgust but one of desire. I don't know how I could tell for sure, but I could. I was about to remove the tube when he said, "No, don't stop!" Vaughn locked the door, came over, and knelt between my legs. We looked at each other with desire, even though we both knew we had no business being together like that.

He said, "Let me help you!" I could manage nothing but "Okay!" He put his left hand on the inner thigh of my right leg, the one that was raised on the desk, and with his other hand, he took control of the test tube. He fucked me with it, and the experience was so intense. I pinched my nipples and, with both hands available at that time, I pushed my breasts together and pushed then up toward my mouth, licking on my own nipples.

I was about to explode, and apparently he could tell that I was about to cum, because he took the test tube out of me and said, "No, I don't want you to cum yet!" He put the test tube up to my mouth and said, "Lick it! Taste yourself for me!" As he held it in place, I placed my hand over his and began to lick my pussy juice off the test tube while we gazed in each other's eyes. I licked it clean, and he gave me a kiss on my lips and sucked on my bottom lip, withdrawing a quick sample of my nectar from it.

He slowly put the test tube back into my pussy and began to fuck me with it again, but this time, he sucked on my breasts for me. I cupped my left one in my hand and fed it to him. He was grateful to have it. After a few moments, I fed him the other one too. He pulled my hips down a little farther on the seat and reclined it so that my ass was exposed just enough for him to finger it.

I couldn't hold back anymore. I came harder than I had ever cum before. I can't be sure, but judging from his reaction, I think he came also, even though his dick never left his pants. He pulled the cum-drenched tube from my pussy and devoured every last drop of it.

For at least ten minutes after that, we were speechless. I sat there recovering from what had just taken place. He stared at me while he ran his fingers through the baby-fine pussy hair on my swollen vagina. I cannot explain how it feels to make love to a person and never have actual inter-course. It was so sexy.

We were still sitting there, basking in the afterglow, the only sounds in the room being the rotating blades of the box fan and voices of coeds walking across campus far below the ajar windows, when a knock came at the door. We both snapped out of our trance instantly and I struggled to get dressed while Vaughn told the dean of the Chemis-try Department that he would be right there. It turns out Vaughn had left the meeting to come retrieve some notes for a proposal he was supposed to give to the rest of the professors in the department and was due to go straight back. I guess the sight of a woman fucking herself with a test tube could throw most any man off track.

He left the room grinning from ear to ear, and I went back to grading papers with a smile on my face as well. I couldn't believe what had happened, but I have never re-gretted it to this very day. Vaughn and I never mentioned it for the rest of my time at State. I remained his assistant and continued to call him Professor Mason.

I am now a chemist for a pharmaceutical company in Texas. Recently, I was going through some old boxes from college, and guess what I found? A 500 ml test tube made out of Pyrex. I wonder where that came from!

The Diary

It had been a long time since I visited my grandparents, and I was excited about spending a couple of days with them for Thanksgiving. When I got off the plane, both of them were waiting for me. With the exception of a few added wrinkles on their faces, they looked exactly like they did when I was a child.

They drove me back to the big country manor where my mother and her three sisters grew up. Once I threw my bags in the bedroom where I would be staying, the one that belonged to my mother as a child, I went down to the kitchen to help Grandma stuff the turkey and bake pies for dinner the next day.

Thanksgiving dinner was going to be great because I would get to see my aunts, their husbands, and all of my cousins. My parents were traveling in Europe, so they were going to have to miss it.

After we finished preparing everything, my grandparents

and I sat in the living room by the fire and talked about the good old days. Grandpa surprised me by having a pizza delivered. I had never even pictured my grandparents eating something that wasn't homemade, much less pizza. Times had really, really changed. There was no denying that.

One thing had remained the same, however, and that was how early they went to bed every night. By 9 P.M., they were both calling the hogs, since they got up around 5 A.M. every morning. They had retired years before but still rose early by force of habit.

I flipped through the channels of the old floor-model television in the living room, the only television in the entire house. They didn't have cable. There were a few sitcoms on, but none of them interested me. I looked through the bookcase in my grandpa's study, hoping to find something interesting to read. All his books were about carpentry, farming, fly-fishing, landscaping, home repair, and things of that nature, so I quickly gave up on the idea.

I quietly went upstairs to my mother's bedroom, undressed, put on a white cotton nightgown, and tried to go ahead and fall asleep. There was no freaking way that was happening, because it was way too early for me.

I was going to hang my garment bag up in her closet, but the closet was packed to the brim with clothing that belonged to her as a teenager. I slipped on my bedroom shoes and went to check and see if there was some space for it in the hallway closet.

I opened the walk-in closet in the hall and found some

space for my bag. The closet had a door in the rear of it that led to the attic. I was mad bored, and since there was nothing to watch on television and nothing to read, I elected to explore the attic instead.

I nudged open the door to the attic stairs, which was hard to open and squeaky, being that no one had been up there in years. After ascending the stairs and finding the pull string for the lightbulb, I was surprised to see there were very few spiderwebs around. However, there was a lot of dust, and I almost turned around in fear my allergies would start acting up.

I was reaching for the string to turn off the light when I noticed an old hope chest in a corner by the window seat. Normally, I am not a nosy person, but something drew me to the chest like a magnet. Besides, my whole point in going up there in the first place was to meddle through family heirlooms and mementos anyway.

I tried to open the chest, but there was a lock on it and the key was nowhere in sight. I shifted through a couple of boxes filled with clothing, cheerleader pom-poms and batons, yearbooks belonging to my mother and her sisters, and all the usual things until I found an old rusty screwdriver.

I used the flat head of the screwdriver to bust the lock on the chest. It didn't take much effort, since the lock was flimsy after so much time. I sat down on the window seat and started pulling things out. There were several photographs of my grandparents when they were younger, pictures of their wedding, pictures of my mother and aunts as children and teenagers, pictures of my great-grandparents and other family members. There were some old lace handkerchiefs, a couple of hand-knitted cardigans, and even a poodle skirt.

Looking at all the old things made me crack up laughing. I couldn't even relate to times like those. For me, growing up had been so different than the way my mother grew up. I guess one day my daughter, if I have one, will be saying the same thing about me.

After beginning to replace everything back in the trunk neatly, I noticed something stuck at the bottom I hadn't noticed the first time around. I yanked on it and got it free. It turned out to be an old book of some sort with no visible name on the cover. The underside of it was sticky, as if something, maybe water, had seeped through the trunk over the years and made it adhere to the lining of the trunk.

I was hoping it was some famous classic novel I could take back down to the bedroom and read until I got sleepy. It wasn't until I opened it up that I realized it was a diary.

The first page said, "This Diary Belongs To," but the name had been smudged, and I couldn't make it out.

I started flipping through it, looking to see if the keeper of the diary signed the pages, but none of them were signed. In fact, only the month and day were at the heading of each page. There was no year written down. I thought that was strange, but since I am not a sleuth or anything, I didn't ponder the fact for very long.

The handwriting was unfamiliar to me, but I knew for sure it wasn't my mother's. I wondered which one of my aunts the diary belonged to. Since I knew it would be inappropriate to read the diary, no matter whose it was, I began to close it so I could put it back. But there was a bookmark in it, and I wanted to see what it said, so I opened it to that particular page.

The bookmark turned out to have a friendship poem imprinted on it, along with a bouquet of flowers. That was not the interesting part, though. Some words caught my eye, and I was shocked.

I sucked his dick, Fingering me, and *I came so hard* seemed to jump right up off the page at me. I was like "DAYUMM-MMMMMMMMM!"

I couldn't prevent myself from reading the whole entry.

July 4th

I saw my Pookie earlier in the day at the Independence Day Parade. He looked so fine in his football uniform. He marched down Main Street with the football team and we, the cheerleaders, followed behind them with the marching band.

Momma wouldn't let me go to the lake with him and the other kids directly after the parade. She made me come home and do all my regular Saturday chores instead. I hurried through them, making sure I would have them all done so she would let me go to see the fireworks.

I managed to get everything done and she told me I could go. I took a long, hot bath and put on some rosewater so I would smell sweet for my Pookie. I put on a blue dress, a white sweater, some white bobby socks, along with my new pair of saddle shoes, and headed down to the lake where the fireworks show was going to be.

When I got there, Pookie and his friends had already been there for hours. They were kind of drunk from drinking the moonshine Pookie's Uncle Willy makes in his homemade still.

I rushed into his arms and he kissed me on my lips, slipping his tongue in my mouth for a brief second. He didn't dare kiss me any more than that in public. He knew if news of it got back to my daddy, we would both be in for a serious whupping.

The fireworks show began at dusk and all the vibrant lights, mixed with the loud bangs as they went off, were breathtaking. We were sitting on blankets by the lake that was surrounded by all the townspeople.

About halfway through the show, Pookie took my hand, rolled a blanket up and stuck it under his arm, and told me to come with him. I let him lead the way and we disappeared deep into the trees where no one could possibly see us.

We found a clearing about 200 yards from the lake and Pookie spread out the blanket on the ground. We could still see the fireworks in the distance yet we had all the privacy we needed.

I told him my mother told me to come straight home after the fireworks ended and he assured me I would be home early enough that I wouldn't get grounded.

Then we started doing the things we couldn't do in public. It wasn't our first time making love because we did it in his daddy's car about a month ago. When I lost my virginity, it hurt at first but then I realized how much I enjoyed it.

Tonight was even better since I was so much more relaxed. We both were. We started out by French kissing. His tongue was a tad bitter from all the moonshine but I loved it just the same. I have always loved kissing him. He is so passionate and domineering.

He unbuttoned my sweater and slowly slid it off me. Then he laid me back on the blanket, undid the top part of my dress, reached behind my back, and unclasped my bra.

After getting my breasts within his grasp, he started sucking on my hard nipples and I was taken aback. My nipples are so sensitive and whenever he sucks them, I can't help but moan from all the pleasure.

I could look up at the sky and see the fireworks bursting in the air as he pushed my dress up, pushed my panties to the side and started fingering me. It hurt a little since my pussy is still somewhat tight. At one point, I almost shrieked out in pain because he tried to stick three fingers inside me at once.

Pookie realized how uncomfortable it was making me and took his fingers out of me. I felt bad about it and told him I wanted to try that thing we have been discussing lately, me giving him a blow job.

He asked me was I sure I was ready to try it and I said yes but that was only partially true. I was nervous but anxious to return the pleasure he gave me when he performed oral sex on me that night in his daddy's car.

I told him to lie down on his back and I unzipped his pants and took out his hard dick. I just stared at it for a few moments at first because I had never taken a really good look at it.

After I built up some confidence, I sucked his dick right there in the woods and I would be lying if I said I didn't relish it. I have the feeling sucking Pookie's dick is going to become a favorite pastime of mine.

I moved my mouth up and down on his dick, taking more and more of it in until I got the whole thing in. Not bad for my first time. He must have found delight in it because he discharged the contents of his balls in my mouth. His hot cum trickled down my throat and while it was not the best-tasting thing in the world, I found it to be quite savory.

He was so out of breath when it was over, I thought we weren't going to be able to do the actual sex act tonight, but he came back strong in a matter of minutes.

I could tell the fireworks show was about over because they seemed to be sending up the big combination ones they always do in the grand finale. I told Pookie maybe we should just go, but he told me how much he wanted to be inside me and I melted.

I lay down again and got in the missionary position so he could stick it in. It went in pretty smoothly, not like the first time when he had to force it in. He started pumping his dick in and out my pussy and lifted up my left leg, holding it up with his shoulder. He took me much harder tonight than before. I guess he figured it was time to take it to the bridge.

The grand finale of the fireworks was amazing, just like the love Pookie and I were making. He kept going and going at it and I was overcome by how long he lasted. One of my girlfriends told me that boys last longer after they cum the first time. I guess she was right.

I came so hard that it scared me. I didn't cum at all the first time we did it and so tonight, I experienced my first orgasm. It was amazing. While Pookie was walking me home, I kept replaying my orgasm over and over again in my mind.

When we got back to the house, he kissed me on my cheek because he knew Daddy was looking out on the front porch through the curtains. I told him I would see him at church tomorrow morn-

ing. I can hardly wait. As Pookie walked off, he turned around and said one day he was going to marry me. This might sound crazy, but you know what? I believe him!

After I finished reading the diary entry, I repeated the word, "DAYUMMMMMMMMMM!"

I couldn't believe one of my aunts had written it. I guess it's always hard to picture people older than me being young and having such experiences.

As I replaced the diary and put all the other things back on top of it, I realized reading it had made my pussy start throbbing. I was so horny and had not a clue what to do. I didn't bring my vibrator or dildo with me on my trip for two reasons. First of all, because I didn't want them to show up on the X-ray machines at the airport and second, because who in the hell plans on masturbating while on vacation at her grandparents' house.

I had to do something, so I closed up the trunk and pushed it back in the corner, grabbed a baton from one of the boxes, pulled the string on the light, and then sat back on the window seat. The only light left in the attic came from the moonlight streaming in through the small square window by the seat and the faint light at the bottom of the stairs emitting from the hallway downstairs.

I pulled my nightgown up, pushed my panties out the way, and started fucking myself with one end of the baton. The rubber end and cold metal created a strange sensation, one that turned me on even more.

I pushed more and more of the baton inside me until no

more would fit comfortably. I spread my legs open wider and starting grinding my hips on to it like it was a big, juicy dick.

I used my free hand to undo the top two buttons of my gown so I could caress my breasts. I pushed my right one up as far as I could and swiped my tongue back and forth across my erect nipple.

This continued on for a good fifteen minutes. The whole time I was imagining the couple in the story who were faceless to me. Yet the woman was obviously one of my mother's sisters. I was dying to know which one.

After playing the whole excerpt from the diary out in my mind and fucking myself royally with the baton, I came like a clap of thunder. I sat there for a couple minutes to regain my normal breathing pattern, which had become shallow. It always does after I cum.

I made sure everything was just like it was before and then tiptoed back down the steps through the closet, shutting the door behind me, and went back to my mother's bedroom.

My grandparents were still sleeping soundly. By that time, it was getting pretty late. I may not have been tired before going up the attic but after masturbating like that, falling asleep came easily.

I woke up the next day still wondering whom the diary belonged to. I devised a plan in my mind to find out.

Thanksgiving dinner went off beautifully, and I had a great time catching up with my aunts and their families. While we sat around reminiscing about the past, I looked at all of them and couldn't picture any of them being the woman from the story. They all seemed so demure.

When they were all putting on their coats and such to leave, I put my plan into action. I told them I had lost my address book and wanted to make sure I had their correct information so I could write to them and call from time to time.

I went from one to the other, asking that all three of them write down their home address and phone number. Later that evening, while I was munching on a slice of Grandma's peach pie that I am totally and undeniably addicted to, I looked at the paper.

All the handwritings were similar. If not for the fact that their names were there, I wouldn't have known who wrote what. Unfortunately, none of the writing samples looked like the writing from the diary.

I figured a person's handwriting does change over the years, and trying to figure the owner of the diary was a lost cause. I was just so amazed by it, but you win some and you lose some.

My grandparents took me to the airport the next day to catch my plane back home. I kissed them good-bye at the gate and told them how much I love them. I promised it wouldn't take me nearly as long to visit again as it did in the past. Grandma surprised me by handing me an index card, telling me she had written down the recipe for her peach pie.

I told her thanks and shoved it in my pocket. They were having final boarding, and I had to rush. I made it onto the plane and found my seat seconds before the pilot put on the Fasten Seat Belt sign.

I flipped through the airline magazine stuffed into the pocket on the back of the seat in front of me but found it dull at best. I had meant to pick up a novel or magazine in the gift shop but got to the terminal too late to risk it.

Once again, I was stuck with nothing to read. Halfway through the flight, I started thinking about my grandma's peach pie. I took the recipe out my pocket to look over the ingredients and directions.

I thought my eyes were playing tricks on me, but I instantly knew they weren't. The handwriting on the index card was identical to the one from the diary, and I was in shock. The woman in the diary, the one whose sexual experience had driven me to the point of masturbation, and ultimately orgasm, was my own grandmother.

It wasn't until a week later, when my mother called from Europe, that I found out Grandma's pet name for Grandpa used to be Pookie. *Dayum, who would have thought it!*

The Seduction

The first time I laid eyes on you, I knew that I wanted to feel you inside me. The first time you kissed me, I thought that I would die. Yet and still, two months and several dates later, we had yet to make love. Partly because you respected me enough to wait and partly because we both wanted the first time to be special.

I decided it was time, since I knew that my body could not settle down for another night's sleep without you. You invaded my every thought. I dreamed of you doing things to me all the time, whether I was stuck in rush-hour traffic or walking down the aisle in the grocery store. The mere thought of you made my juices flow. I was determined to make the night special, something neither one of us would ever forget.

It was a Friday evening about 6 P.M. when you left your office, tired but elated that the workweek was over. We didn't have any plans and hadn't spoken, even by telephone, for the past few days, which is why the note in the white envelope with lace trim on your windshield took you by total surprise.

As you lifted the note from under the wiper, you could smell the scent of my perfume, all too familiar to you now, breeze past your nose in the brisk October wind. It was a cold evening, but I had plans to warm you up.

You opened the note and read it:

Hey Baby,

I know we didn't have plans for tonight, but I have a surprise for you. You have to come to me in order to find out what it is. A friend of mine asked me to house-sit her new home while she is out of town getting her furniture. It is kind of way out, so I drew you a map on the back of this note.

If you want to experience a night of lovemaking that will stimulate all of your senses and allow me to pamper your entire body as well as your mind, CUM TO ME! Don't bring anything but your sexy ass. Hurry up, baby, because I need you.

<SMOOCHES>
Zane

You smile as you see the imprint of my lips, in red lipstick, at the very bottom of the note. You can feel your dick getting hard in your pants as you lick your lips and drive off to begin our adventure together.

The house was indeed hard to find but you accomplished the deed and pulled up in the secluded driveway about an hour later. It was a nice little cottage way out in the country, surrounded by trees. As you got out of the car, you couldn't help but notice how quiet it was. You thought you heard an owl way off in a distant tree as you approached the front door.

When you got to the door, there was a piece of paper attached to it saying:

Roses are red
Violets are blue
Tonight's the night
For me and you

Come in my love
And you will find
In front of you
A glass of wine

You turned the doorknob and opened the door and entered into my idea of romance. The entire house appeared empty, for there was no furniture as far as you could see. Every room was lit up by flickering pillar candles, all vanilla scented, in various sizes and shapes. In the living room, you could see the fire I had built for us. A single glass of white Zinfandel was sitting on the hearth. As you picked it up and began to sip on it, you noticed a white silk scarf and another note lying beside it. You read it:

Quench your thirst
With this glass of wine
Relax a bit
And unwind

Then cover your eyes
Give in to me
I will cum for you
And help you to see

A faint laugh escapes your lips as you finish up your glass of wine. Then you cover your eyes with the silk scarf without hesitation, wondering what I have in store for you next.

As soon as you complete your task, you hear the sounds of Kenny G coming from upstairs. Because of the music, you don't hear my light footsteps descending the stairs and walking up behind you. Once I am very close, you can smell my sweet perfume. You begin to say hello to me, but I reach around in front of you and cover your lips with one of my fingers and say, "Shhhhhh!"

I felt we had talked enough, and I wanted the night to be all about the other senses. I had always wanted to get to know you three ways. I knew you mentally, and now, I wanted to get to know you physically and orally.

I put my hand up to your chest and could feel your heartbeat. I took your right hand and placed it over my heart, and you noticed that my chest was bare. I was already completely nude. For a brief moment, we admired the life emitting from both of us as two heartbeats became one.

I took you by the hand and led you up the stairs to the bathroom where a candlelit bubble bath was waiting. As I began to undress you, you could smell the essence of the rose petals scattered over the top of the bathwater. I undressed you very slowly, admiring every inch of you as it was revealed.

Once you were undressed, I bit my bottom lip with excitement as I took in the splendor of your dick with my eyes. I helped you up the two steps that led to the huge whirlpool garden tub and guided you in. I sat down in front of you with my legs over your thighs and began to bathe you with a soft bath sponge. I began with the top of your head, then moved on to your chest, your back, your shoulders, your arms, your dick, your thighs, and your knees. Finally, I bathed your feet.

One at a time, I took your toes into my mouth and suckled on them, enjoying the reaction on your face and the low moans coming from your sexy lips as the water vibrating out of the whirlpool jets tingled our skin.

When I was done, I stood you up, helped you out of the tub, and began to dry you off with a soft cotton bath towel. I quickly discarded that option and decided to lick you dry instead. Systematically, I licked the remaining water off every inch of you. I remember thinking that I had never in life tasted something so delicious.

I traced a trail with my tongue around each one of your nipples and down the middle of your chest to your belly button. I got down on my knees and licked each one of your thighs and knees and then turned you around so

I could lick the back of your thighs and knees. I took the thickness of my tongue and lapped up all the droplets on the cheeks of your ass, licked the entire crease, and then stuck my tongue deep inside your asshole. I could feel you shiver as I turned you around again and took your balls gently into my mouth, suckling the water droplets off of them as well.

What I really craved to lick all over was your beautiful dick, and I did just that. With you still blindfolded by the silk scarf, I devoured every inch of you while you stood there and dick-fed me for the first time. As you ran your fingers through my damp hair that smelled of the strawberry shampoo I used that morning, I took my time enjoying my candy treat. I arched my neck back so that I could take you all in for what seemed like endless moments. When I sensed you were about to explode, I reached up and removed the blindfold from your eyes, and you saw me for the first time that day and the first time ever in the nude.

As your eyes adjusted to the light, you saw me sitting there on my knees with my cherry-colored lips surrounding your dick, my nipples harder than diamonds, and water trickling down my bare back onto my succulent ass. There among the candlelight, with Kenny G still emitting through the master bedroom door into the bathroom, you looked down and removed the hair from in front of my eyes just in time to look deep into them as you came into my mouth for the very first time.

We both lost control as your warm, sweet nectar trick-led down my throat and lined my insides with your essence. After I had partaken of every drop, I stood up and whispered in your ear that it wasn't over yet, and the only response you could muster was "Dayummmmm!"

I took you by the hand and led you into the bedroom, where you spotted the single piece of furniture in the whole house, a king-size sleigh bed covered with black satin sheets. Candles also lighted the bedroom, and the single white rose I had gotten for you was lying on a pillow in the center of the bed. I laid you down upon the satin sheets. As lightning began to invade the room from over the horizon, tracing both our bodies with its presence, I took the single rose, began at the top of your head, and moved it all the way down the center of your body. I paused it for a moment at the tip of your nose so that you could admire the essence of it. You laughed a little as the rose petals tickled your skin.

I reached over to the side of the bed onto the floor and returned with a bottle of scented body oil and two more silk scarves. I tied your hands to the headboard and proceeded to give you a full body massage, working my small delicate hands over your smooth skin. I massaged you from head to toe, making sure that you were totally relaxed. Then I reached over and got the bottle of honey I had waiting beside the bed and squeezed a few drops over both of my breasts. I fed them to you, one at a time, as you lay there with your head on the pillow.

After breast-feeding you for a few moments, I took the honey and squeezed some all over my vagina and ass. Then, I climbed on top of your face in the sixty-nine position and felt you begin to suck on my clit with a desire no other man had ever shown. I poured some honey on your dick and began to lick it all off, making long, circular strokes around the shaft with the tip of my tongue. We sucked on each other for a long time, and the CD player kicked over to the next one in sequence, Maxwell's *Urban Hang Suite,* as we both had orgasm on top of orgasm.

We devoured each other until we were both completely exhausted, our mouths were sore, my pussy was swollen, and your dick had the kind of tender soreness that comes about when too many orgasms are reached at one time. We both fell asleep just like we were positioned, with my pussy on your face and the head of your dick in my mouth, your hands still tied to the bed.

The music eventually faded out sometime during the night, and all the candles burned completely down, leaving only the lightning flashes and the distant claps of thunder to invade our private paradise.

In the morning, you awoke to find your hands untied and me standing there with a silver tray, holding the breakfast I had prepared to serve in bed. We fed each other the chocolate-covered strawberries, grapes, and freshly baked blueberry muffins with our fingers.

There, in the first sunlight of the day, you and I made love for the very first time, and I finally got my wish. I felt you inside of me. Now, years later, with our fifth wedding anniversary approaching, we both smile at each other with the secret only the two of us know every time we visit my friend in the country, the godmother of our firstborn son.

Whenever life seems to pale in comparison, we remember the night I first seduced you and welcome the challenge of making our next night of passion top every one before it. Guess what, baby? You never, ever disappoint me.